ON THE GANGA GHAT explores the play of life as it unfolds in Benares, the cherished ultimate destination of millions of Indians, the holy city to die in. And so it is that to the Ganga ghats in Benares come rajahs and princes from Bengal; beggars; Katiawari merchants; courtesans; crooks; simpletons and charlatans—seeking meaning in life, or redemption in death. No less varied are the creatures of the Benares themselves: the gentle, brahmchari Madhoba and his Mohini—a feminine presence, "something more than a goddess, a woman"; Bhim, the sage parrot; the Brahmini cow Jhaveri Bai bounteous concubines like Nanna; hard-swearing, mantra-chanting sadhus laughing at the foibles of others.

On the Ganga Ghat is a collection of eleven stories, and marks Raja Rao's return to the short story after a gap of over a decade. The prose is exquisite: chiselled, sparse yet evocative. The result is mesmerising.

RAJA RAO was born in Mysore in 1909 and went to Europe at the age of nineteen, researching in literature at the University of Montpellier and at the Sorbonne. He wrote and published his first stories in French and English. His five novels—and three collections of short stories—have all won wide and exceptional international acclaim, including the Sahitya Akademi Award and the 1988 Neustadt International Prize for Literature.

Raja Rao is now at work revising the next two volumes of the *Chessmaster* trilogy.

Also by
Raja Rao

The Serpent and the Rope
Comrade Kirillov
The Chessmaster and His Moves
Kanthapura
The Cat and Shakespeare

RAJA RAO

ON THE GANGA GHAT

ORIENT PAPERBACKS
A Division of Vision Books Pvt. Ltd.
New Delhi • Bombay

"Water Does Not Flow"
SRI ATMANANDA GURU

Rs. 60.00

ISBN-81-222-0149-0

© Raja Rao

1st Published in 1993 by
Orient Paperbacks
(A Division of Vision Books Pvt. Ltd.)
Madarsa Road, Kashmere Gate, Delhi-110 006

Printed in India at
Kay Kay Printers, Delhi-110 007

Cover Printed at
Ravindra Printing Press, Delhi-110 006

To The Reader

These stories are so structured that the whole book should be read as one single novel.

All persons and places are not true—but real.

There is a glossary at the end for those who need any particular name or word explained. Yet, it must be said, why not just flow with the Ganges.

Raja Rao

I

"*P*alanquin, Palanquin, leave the way, ho, for His Honour, the Palanquin" — this is how we should have been received at Mughal Sarai station, but we're met by self-selling, high-turban-adjusting taxi drivers, their chariots betoken of a forgotten dignity. "Saab, paisa, money," said the coolies, trying to get rid of us before the customary hagglings began, thus again that they'd not have to bear their burdens too long. "Saab, the Gaya Express is coming soon." Here however two curs introduced themselves, noses up and ears straight, to watch the argument — they also were going to get something from these new customers. One, with long hanging pips, was trying to edge the other, a leansome male, lest there should be the possibility of a gift. "Even a cur in Benares is blessed," said the great Sri Sankara, and who can say what these curs were, what ancient souls reborn for their ultimate salvation on the Ganga banks. The bullocks too, from a neighbouring cart, waved their ears. They heard this haggle as if they again would profit from some ultimate benefit. In Benares everything — bullock carts, rags, human excreta (in cones or flat), fallen wayside hay, tree-tops, burnt charcoals, abandoned bus horns, beggars, ugly names on worn walls (may be of politicians) — everything, everything benefits from all acts — for no act here has any consequence. An action must have cause and effect. In

Benares there seems no reason for a cause, thus the result is, no effect. No act breeds an act. And so eternity, the bent meaning of the river.

But night, the all-pervading immemoriality that the earth gives herself for her cogitations, it too was an observant of this haggle. In the silence of the trees a monkey or two woke up. They breathed heavily and went back to slumber. This simian heavy breath created a cry from the hanging bats, and these again thought the Calcutta Mail, which they knew day after day from its raucous, diesel whistle, and from the harsh Punjabi accents of its travellers or the rich Bengali ones — they knew that the haggle would go on. The whole night was there for the chase and the hang-to, and, by dawn sweet sleep would come. The midnight hagglers come by the Calcutta Mail and so they are rich. (Even the monkeys by now knew of the air-conditioned coaches.) And where the rich are, the cur and the bullocks — may be even the motor engines of mathematically conditioned reflexes — had known there's always a fight.

"Fifteen rupees to Benares, Saab, and look at my brand new taxi." Paul to whom this was addressed looked wistfully at the much-torn top and the flabby tyres of the noble vehicle arrayed before us.

"Fourteen rupees and eight annas, sir," said the young Sikh driver who spoke some English. "You want to go to the Metropolitan Hotel."

"Go you," said an elderly, round-faced and beturbaned colleague. "They're going to the university. With all your learning, can't you see they're students?"

"Shut up, old fellow. My uncle has gone to Canada and he was there twenty years before you were born. I know what books are. I have studied up to the Matric."

"Yes, yes, you study up to the Matric," took up the elder, "and you drive those rotten taxis, those newcomers that go *phut* every second twist you give to the wheel. Look, sir, look at my old model. I take marriage processions in it, often. And you students, with all your books and luggage, you always take me."

"No doubt, no doubt. You have a regular nuptial palanquin," said the youngster with his uncle gone to Canada, and that decided us.

"Paul," I said, "let us take this palanquin." And Paul laughed. The old 1939 model Ford was exactly like a large bullock cart. Its sides (being a larger, and so, older a car) indeed were more torn than those of the smaller Indian ones, made, so to say, but the other day.

"You won't take that palanquin, sir," said the young man in English almost belligerently. "The old man does not even have a car licence."

"We take that palanquin," I declared, and when we asked the coolies to pile in our luggage, the coolies were pleased. They always liked this Moti Ram, the driver. "He's a good man, sir," they assured us, tying up the luggage on the top and back. "A father of many children. And he's also such a good drummer. You must hear him at Holi."

"Drummer," said the young man with Canadian connections, "his children beat their stomachs for a drum. That's how hungry they are. Poor kids," he said and turned, tired, to some new customers. This time they were Punjabis, and they could speak the same lingo. And there was a lovely child with the father and the mother. There would be no haggling with them. Five rupees, the traveller said, and eight they agreed upon, and thus they entered the car and drove away, before our car had taken its breath to make its august first move.

"How much for your palanquin?" I asked smiling.

"Oh, the Sahib has travelled much, one can see. The other Sahib is an European. Thus you know what to give a poor man."

Remembering our Indian companion's friendly advice earlier in the train, Paul said, "Make sure, Raja, what he wants." I liked our palanquin and its owner. I felt the night had heard enough hagglings. There was even now a large crowd on the platform, the Calcutta Mail was still watering. The vendors were busy, and there was something altogether unconvincing about the high overbridge, the lit train, and the night-alive crowd. The world is indeed the city seen in a mirror, and, upside down.

Strange to say the coolies did not haggle. They just took their wages, and a modest tip, and walked away, their red turbans on their head as if they were going back to dream. The train truly was the dream that ran through their nights. The multiple languages, shapes, and colours of the pilgrims, from the guttural Tamil speakers to the nasal Bengalis — it all seemed too variegated to be concrete. The Mughal Sarai coolies must be among the wisest men in the world. They see more humanity than at any other railway station on this globe. Five hundred million Hindus are their clients, and not just that: their ancestors have come too, to this same Benares, life after life, and thus have established a pilgrim link between man and man. Why should one be born near Mughal Sarai, and be a coolie? In what past life was there a desire to serve pilgrims who go to the Ganga? Mother Ganga always knows. "I tell you brother, if Mother Ganga did not decide, there would be no Sita Ram or this Bhaiya Ram carrying luggages on Mughal Sarai railway platform. We carry beddings, nightjars, tiffin carriers, punkhas, canes, cradles, vessels, silver tumblers, coconuts, and gold on our shoulders — sometimes we even carry the ashes of the dead that the mourners bring in red-cloth baskets, we carry the trousseau of the newly wed, we also carry the last possession of those who come to the Ganga to die, old men who know that time is come to give their last breath away, by the Ganges. Such our trade. We revere it. Our fathers have done it. Some say our ancestors were thugs: they worshipped Bhavani, and betimes strangulated travellers for the pleasure of the Goddess. Others say, before the rails came, we were the palanquin bearers of the rich. We have always had to do with travellers. Brother, our job is service to the pilgrim. The great God who sits on the other side of the Ganges, he alone knows what we are, where we go. O, that donkeyson Punjab Express is already there. Run," they say, as they rush up the gangway.

Life is so mysterious. Why should you, coolie with a number — 87, 54 or 49 — stitched on your shirt, alone carry our luggage? Why not one whose number is 55, 31 or 48? What connection of stars linking one with the other, Jupiter with Mercury or Saturn squaring the moon, have created this situation that Bhaiya Ram, Bhagat Ram or Durga Das, coolies of Mughal Sarai, carry our luggage and never will we see them again? How could this be? And the monkeys that were disturbed by our hagglings, the bats that were irritated and the two curs — yes, those two curs, Paul and I will never meet again. Only the Ganges flows, Mother Ganges carrying our memories away. Who could, Lord, who could carry the memory of the millions and millions that have been born since the beginnings began and where have all the dog-and-man-meetings, the bat and the travellers' links, the coolie-and-the-pilgrim-contacts gone? Why was Paul here and he from Chapel Hill, North Carolina, son of my friend Bert who sent him with me to India — a graduation present! And who, I? And who indeed was this Moti Ram driving us into the wild darkness of the night? Where was he taking us? Did he have a licence? Did he know the road to Raj Ghat College? Silence in India is always wise. But over there on the Ganges bank it seems to sparkle. The darkness yields slowly to an unearthly luminescence. Man, do you know you would know if only you knew you knew? And Mother Parvathi presides over it all.

Anna Purné Sada Purné
Shankar Prana Vallabhé...
Bhikshandéhicha Parvathi.

O filled with essence and ever in plenitude,
Beloved to life of Shankara himself,
O Parvathi, give me alms.

Yes, Parvathi alone gives. It is through Her we know Him. How could we know we know if the door of darkness remained unopened? She opens. She hears your cry, son. She hears because you weep childless, woman. She hears because you've lost your son, old father. In fact, hearing itself is She. And when hearing is just hearing nobody hears: so He is.

Moti Ram, our driver, indeed bore a palanquin. His car made a large variety of noises as we scudded and rode on, startled sometimes by the bright eyes of bullocks from the incoming carts. And then night again slipped by and enveloped all of hearing. Only once a horse-cart jostled past us with a chattering group of travellers inside, and the horse was getting a nice lash for every other breath — they had to catch, the travellers had to, the Gaya Express. Gaya is where the Buddha attained enlightenment. Kanthaka, his horse, was that which had arisen life after life, only to be the horse on whom the Buddha would ride to go to his enlightenment.

"Moti Ram," I said, "how many children have you?"

"Three, sir," he answered ever so reverentially. "I had four. And one of them died."

"Died of what, Moti Ram?"

"He died of death, sir, that is all. One morning we awoke, and found him dead."

"Was there some black magic behind it, you think?"

"Who would do magic against a grave good boy? He used to carry fuel from the fuel shop to the Ganga banks for cremations. He had seen too many souls die."

"No, he must have died of something."

"Well, sir, we must all die of something. Does it matter the manner he was taken away? His time was come, and he was taken away."

"And the other three. What do they do?"

"One works at a primary school. He is a peon there. And he takes letters to your Raj Ghat College sometimes. He has seen that great Mahatma, Krishnamurti, sir. The Mahatma probably knows you."

"Yes, Moti Ram, I have met him once or twice. But I haven't been to Raj Ghat College for many, many years — in fact for fifteen years."

"Oh yes, sir," mumbled Moti Ram to himself as if he had made a grave mistake in etiquette, and fell back to silence. The silence now simply whirled as solid space, as if the earth were but a turning top on Shiva's palm. The earth whirls in the pure silence of akasha, of space essence. Man whirls with it too and his words become silences. As the Ganges dissolves all acts of man so does silence dissolve all of speech. Man is never more a pilgrim than when silence carries him from darkness into light. Mother Ganga bends as a moon, as a Crescent Moon, by Benares. Look at that still string of electric lights, a string through the awake night which seems to deepen the river's truth. Once in a while a lean tongue of flame flares up — some dead whose body was being slowly turned to ash, which would finally be dissolved into the Ganga. Pyre, and pyre again, became prominent as we neared the river. The flames seemed so alive, the only nightly action in this visible universe. The string of lights seemed but reflections seen from the other side. Who were they, the one, two, or three, which had died, banker, virgin, retired police constable or Maharaja? And the yogis must watch these pyres as they open their eyes after their midnight meditations. The pyre makes death alive. He who has seen a body burn, knows he will never die.

The Dalhousie bridge burst like wide laughter while a funeral is passing by. The girders rippled off their silences but at each rib they seemed to get merrier. The Dalhousie bridge was not laughing at anyone. He was laughing at the immensities he linked, and his ever light burden. And he too having served millions of pilgrims, will one day be broken by flood or war, and he too will fall into the Ganga, though the steel had come from Cumberland or Glasgow. There's hope for every thing on earth, man, beast, and iron ore.

One saw neither palace, temple nor minaret of mosque — one only saw the curve of the Ganga. Was Benares a city or a Sanskritic statement? Did not a million people live there? Were there not colleges, universities, judicial buildings, town hall, the palaces of the rich, where were they all? From the bridge there was nothing seen but the sacred river turning, bending in her legendary crescent form, and sprays of gathering upper luminosities, and then the stars. The silence was alarming. The Ford suddenly turned to the right (for, by now, the bridge was crossed over) and cautiously we entered the new suburbs of the city. Walls of plaster, mud or brick, nuts, villas, and thatchments — there was not a human breath anywhere. At the railway crossing we saw the only thing awake, the red light, and we entered darkness again. The unreal and the real are so co-adjacent in Benares you lose trace of the one, while you are wholly with the other. Was there a Raj Ghat College? Did Moti Ram really know it? How could one trust a man with his peasant turban, his big belly, silver bangles on his arm, as Moti Ram? Did he have a licence? Did he too have a Thug ancestor?

Through listless curves and roads without end, which suddenly opened on broader roads, and narrow dips, we emerged at a gate. Moti Ram stopped the car, and a cur started barking. Moti Ram went, opened the gate wide, and the cur raised his voice higher. Who dare come in on this stark night? What man dare, on the Ganges bank, break this deadly darkness? The cur was indeed Yama's dog for he never stopped howling. Through many twists and chugs we came to another gate. We saw almost no houses or huts. Only trees everywhere. There's the terror of Bhavani in every wood. Someone shouted in the night.

"Who's there?"

"Guests for you, Jagat Ram. This is Moti Ram of the Taxi, speaking. Father of Sachit Ram."

"Guest? What guest?" the dialogue started.

"What do I know? Name, country? They are Sahibs and that's all I know."

"How can I open the door," said the voice, switching on a garden light, "without knowing their names?"

"Say Raja Rao," I said.

"Raja Rao Sahib," cried Moti Ram as if he were announcing a king.

"I know no Raja Rao," cried back the voice.

"They're big people," assured Moti Ram, "very big people, from far off countries. There's also a Sahib there."

"What Sahib?" shouted Jagat Ram slowly coming towards us. His dog continued to bark sharing the dialogue. "Who are they anyway?" He knew we were not what we were supposed to be.

"I've written to the Principal. I have sent a telegram. They are expecting me," I said, getting out of the car. I was tired, and I did not expect this dialogue ever to stop. The dog's bark became viler, we were obviously not wanted.

"Oh," said Jagat Ram speculating about me from top to bottom. "Oh, you are the guests the college office was speaking about. They knew somebody was coming. But they knew neither his name nor his address. What could I do? They said, the clerk said, 'Somebody may come in tonight. May be a Sahib too,' they remarked. Even the emissaries of Yama himself can come. Could I let any one in? Well, however, you are there. Come in." And he pushed the gate sideways. From then on Jagat Ram never spoke a word. He opened up the guest room, a smallish white washed room with two beds, a soiled table, and proudly showed us the bathroom. Yes, we had a private bathroom, western style. The dog stood outside examining the newcomers. Now and again she would suddenly twist her tail and howl. She was not sure her master should be so trusting. "Master, do be careful, you never know."

Meanwhile Jagat Ram was giving us bed sheets and mosquito curtains and pillow cases. Moti Ram brought in the luggage. He stood there on the veranda, as if he had accomplished a holy job. And that was the end of the story.

"You never told me about drums?" I said.

"To the drummer night is like a drum. One hears the beats. You know that's why Lord Shiva has the drum in his hand. He dances in the crematorium, you remember. To beat a leather instrument with God-given hands is easy. But to beat drum that Shiva's silence become sound could only be the gift of Mother Parvathi. He alone beats the drum true, who knows he's never there."

"How wonderful," I remarked hiding my utter clumsiness. "Is there anywhere I can hear you, Moti Ram?"

"No sir, I beat my drum at home only at prayer time. I beat it that the Lord remove my sins. Every beat rubs off a little of my heavy karma." I had no words. I gave Moti Ram ten rupees (eight for the ride and two as baksheesh, I said jokingly), and as he left the door and walked through the garden to the gate, I remembered I would never, never see him hereafter. How auspicious it would be to take the Calcutta Mail, again.

Even after the car had left the dog never stopped barking. After we got into bed, he seemed to remember some forgotten ill we had done to him, and would slowly whine, and suddenly give a bark. Had we done him some harm in another life? Who knows? Every event of life has a double meaning. There is no accident in existence. Yet there is the miracle of chance. To know why you lie on a shaky charpai in this damp building, in what is perhaps the Raj Ghat College Guest House but is, as it were, a nowhere of anywhere, is to ask the question: Who made this rope that wove the charpai? And the tree, the timbers from which the charpai was made? Whence came they? What destiny brought the rope and the string together, and I and Paul to Benares? Event is always single, simple. Event is action without object.

II

Bhim, the parrot, is among the eldest of the kingdom. Lean at the neck (much hair having fallen during these many decades), and with a wisp of white hood, he moves with natural serenity. He seems to have such privileged freedom of movement across the sky of Benares that even the vultures give way to him. His nest is on the neem tree — that old, wind-twisted and tall neem — just where the Dasi lane ends, and the boats come up for people to have a quick look at the Dashashwamedh Ghat and high up, an ever-ordained hole, as it were, exists for Bhim. The story goes (and any boatman worth his salt will tell you) that Bhim and his wife Rupvati have lived here for over fifty years — that is, since the time of the Delhi Durbar until today, and this is till about two or three years ago and the China war — Bhim and Rupvati always moved about with the august marks of princes. They bear a large litter, sometimes of four, sometimes of five, so people thereabouts say, and at least three or four live on. Once in a while a vile vulture used to swoop in or some over-courageous school boy would go and catch the little one, in the deeps of the night, with a torch, and no amount of cries would drive the vicious intruder down.

But since a few years something has happened. Every time a boy wants to go up, he falls off the tree before he is even up to the level of the first veranda of the Bindu

House, to the right. Once, twice, thrice, this happened and people in the Bindu House and the Dasi lane now know that some Siddha has come to live on the neem tree. Often women, when they wake up on a moonlit night, and go to the veranda to contemplate the broad river and the silver of her murmurings, a sudden wind seems to shift on top of the neem tree and one hears, as it were, the sound of a mantra. *Hum hum humumm* it seems to say, with a grave and a ruminant voice. The voice is not human nor is it that of a bird. It certainly is divine, luminescent. Anyhow, from then on Bhim and Rupvati have lived undisturbed and bear their little ones with absolute hope. All little chicks do not survive in Benares nor do all mother birds in Benares have a Siddha to protect them. The little ones grow up and multiply and even today the bird catchers of Benares (and there are none more wicked in this wicked world, I tell you), they say to you, "This is the Bhim-Rupvati breed" just by the ring at the neck, and a sort of pearly mist over the eyes. The colour of the ring is yellow but more close to sapphire than to ochre — there's more green in it than gold. The eyes of Bhim are somewhat small but Rupvati has eyes large as an eight-anna but, and she rolls them with fire. Rupvati must not be easy to live with, yet sometimes when Bhim stands on one leg on some branch of the tree — and this any pilgrim can see — Rupvati sits on another branch and contemplates her lord with devout attention.

Sadhus throw Bengal gram towards the couple but Bhim and Rupvati do not eat all the gram that's offered to them, which explains why near the tree you have such a collection of madhu-birds and sparrows, which get a feast as few birds get anywhere in this wide and bent Benares. And the ants have such a feast too that they have a permanent nest in the tree, and you can see them pass along the trunk down and go towards the Bindu House where they always find sugar from pilgrim kitchens. The Jains will tell you that never do you find so many ants on a tree as on this neem, and some knowing people say, of course because it's of Bhim or maybe it's because of the mighty mantra-intoning Siddha. But the women who sell clay-pots round the corner and who have lived on the lane for so long say there's a story of a Queen, rich and splendid in her beauty, who came to Benares sometime in the time of our grandfathers and drowned herself under that very tree. She was unhappy, and she thought a Ganges death were better than a palace rot. So she slipped through the palace guards, warded off her pursuers (in those days you rode on horseback a great deal, even women did), and she and her maid-companion both came here when the river was in floods and they jumped one after the other into the flow. The fisherman found her floating the next day by Rajghat. They called her, just to give her a name, Prabhavathi, and in the lane they still say, "By Prabhavathi's stone," meaning a little rock by the ghats where Prabhavathi is believed to have come and sat contemplating the river, and when she disappeared a rock suddenly appeared, and that is why in the land of Benares where no stones grow, why this rock astonishingly emerges. True or untrue, the potters will also tell you that a few years after Bhim, the parrot, came to live there, so the elders said, another parrot was seen evening after evening sitting on the Prabhavathi stone. And of course Bhim was Prabhavathi, and her companion (who soon joined him) was born as Rupvati. The fact that Rupvati lives with such arrogance is simple: she was not so much devoted to God as to her queen. And as she jumped into the river, she still continued to feel the pride of her palace surroundings, bells and carpets and elephant-trumpetings, and the high presence of her companions of honour. And the Rajas of Vikramapur, who heard of all this, came royally to Benares, built a square platform around the neem, smeared the stone with ochre, and gave the tree a golden pole (with a Kalasa-mount) and a flag with their peacock insignia. Thus Prabhavathi is, as you see, still in her own kingdom.

Now, the little parrots of Bhim can people the Benares high trees with such sacred namings and songs. The Bhim parrots have one virtue. They never steal. They never learn cinema songs. You can make them take the name of Ram and this they will repeat with delight. And many a Zamindar's wife has carried a Bhim parrot from Benares — and in fine-worked Muradabadi bell-metal cages — to Calcutta or Agra and some have carried them even to Rajasthan. The truth about these parrots is also that they die quickly if they go to the wrong house — a black-marketeer or an unprofessional prostitute, a bribe-loving police officer or a British Official's dancing and drinking wife. One good English lady even took a Bhim parrot to England and he came again and again in her dream and said, "Send me back home, send me back home," and some Indian coming back is said to have brought back the parrot, and let him fly off on the Dasi Lane Ghat. Nobody saw this but it is rumoured the vultures fell on him immediately — such the smell of the evil-touched among birds — anyway he died in Benares, did the London-returned parrot, and this makes it better for rebirth. Who knows, he may have been among the later litters of Bhim and Rupvati.

When Bhim stands on his one leg, the other strictly drawn to his belly-downs, all the world can see that the sparrow and the madhu-bird, and even a vulture or two will come and sit on the other branches, and if by chance you hear a sharp voice or cry, it's because some unwanted rascal has tried to sneak in near this assembly, and the vultures will not have him do so.

The vulture Krodha is a tame old thing, too tame and too old except to catch a fish here and there, or peck at the remains of a carcass. Krodha was seen by man at least since the last twenty years — so people say, since a year or two after Mahatma Gandhi was assassinated. He came, did Krodha, to the Dasi Ghat, an unknown as it were, for he appeared, truth to speak, from nowhere. The Dasi Ghat has few corpses to offer you, while the muslim weavers' quarters on the other side are so full of hide and flesh and fish. Why then here among pilgrims and potters and grave shaven widows? Some vultures do carry off babies, that is true, and Dasi Ghat was no better than any. And of course in the Bindu house and Rati mansion and the Bishembhar Palace (of the Rajas of Bhume) you have so many puling little things. You flop down, catch, and rise and rush off to the Ramnagar bank of the river. But Krodha is a hard task master on himself. He would rather carry a lamb or a cock than a human baby. He felt this way since he saw a baby carried off and it cried so much and beat its hands so fiercely, that five of them had to come and finish off the baby. And human flesh anyway does not taste as good, as say, goose flesh.

Now Krodha has many problems. He has an itch in the neck and a very acute pain on the bend of the back. He took mustard shoots from the fields to cure himself, and even fasted for three or four days, but nothing lessened his pain. However, coming here one day by accident — he was chasing a fish, and he was swooping down, when he saw Bhim. He brought back the fish and ate him on the neem tree. The itch in the neck somehow stopped for a moment. He came again and again, and the pain only stopped when Bhim was standing on his one solitary leg. Usually when Krodha came, the other birds, sparrows and madhu birds, rushed away in fear. But little by little they too began to have assurance of themselves. The fact is Krodha is too crude to know of the Siddha. Everybody cannot know the Siddha, and even among the potters only a few can hear that mantra-like humming of the nights, *Hum...Hum....Hum.* You think sound can be heard because you've ears. I tell you, you can only hear what your ears hear, there are so many many sounds in Benares that your ears cannot even smell of, leave alone see. A sound is like this. It can be thick, or thin, low, minor, or even minion. At each level you have a special ear to hear, that is, if you can hear. If you eat too much onion or carcass or butcher's scrap or steal the manes' offerings from crows or the grain — gifts from cows or peck into gutters like some low birds do, you are out of your circle.

In fact there are two definite circuits in Benares — the outer and the inner. The inner is so clear. It passes from the Dufferin bridge past the main post-office, and skirting the Hindu High School, runs straight down to the kutcheries by the Brahma Bazar Road, and from then on, meandering, you could reach the University campus city — those to the right belong to one caste, to the left the other. To the left you have the weavers, the untouchables, the hide — sellers, the prostitute houses (of the poor and the accidental), and to the right you have the rajas, the concubines, the pilgrims, and the temples — and the river. The vultures of the right do not eat with the vultures of the left — there are strict rules not only about eating but about mating. You have on the right the vultures born life after life feeding on the fishes, the thrown-off meats of pilgrims, and even a good carcass or two. It depends on whose it is. But on the left you must eat all sorts of things, and even share a buffalo with crows or a host of curs. The vulture's cry to the left is like a policeman's whistle, sharp and one-noted, but the vultures of the right have long drawn notes, as if they were gentlemen accustomed to wait on Zamindars. And the two provinces are so clearly drawn that the two types of vultures — the vultures of the left and the vultures of the right — never invade each other's domains. That's the law. And the vultures, you may know, are great obeyers of the law.

This is not always so true of the sparrows. These tiny commonplace populace of Benares are so mixed up in their mediocrities that they eat anywhere, and they mate anywhere, and in fact they peck at any grain, funeral grain, or pilgrim-leavings. They however marry only from the sparrows of the ghat sides, exception being made to those of Ramnagar, on the other bank. For reasons of bird-laws the Ramnagar side is counted as holy. The sparrows too follow the pilgrims sometimes when they make their sixty-league circumbulation of Benares. They go in groups and return by evening to their nests on the Dasi-Ghat or the Hanuman Ghat side. The peculiarity however of the the Benares sparrows is this: they are fearless. Commonplace they may be but proud they are. The story goes that once when Sri Rama was crossing the Ganges a sparrow stood on a side, and swore allegiance of all the sparrows to the Lord.

"Howso?" asked Sri Rama, the fount of compassion. "Howso, Bhagirathi?" for that was the name of the sparrow. "Because," said the sparrow, "once one of our race was born in Janaka's kingdom. Great was the peace and luxury in the land of Devi Sita's father. The sages were honoured and you only heard the murmur of mantras come out from every housetop. And when Janaki the holy one went to the river to bathe, and her housemaids were all busy arranging her clothes on the bank, Sita Devi was so enchanted with the waters she went swimming. Now on the other side of the river was a Rakshasha spirit whose deepest desire was to have cast an eye on Sita Devi bathing for once, and thus Sita would not be Sri Rama's spouse, and there would therefore be no Ramayana. When this monster rose on his bloody bed all the sparrows were frightened, and we on this side did perform an act simple. We flew in wide formations swinging ourselves like a large swap of song which comes back on itself, and the longer Sita Devi stayed in the waters the greater the number of sparrows that joined us on this sky-curtaining flight. So Sita Devi when she saw this called me, Bhagirathi, and said: 'Bird, what festival of yours is this?' 'O none, Princess, but that ogre there has decided there would be no Ramayana, that is, if he could just sight you, as you take your bath, so Sri Rama would not wed you. We know the Lord is born to liberate man from evil. We have woven a net of illusion for the ogre not to see you. Lady, we know you're the daughter of the earth and the Mother of mankind.

Devi, we are but humble protectors of the Queen-born-of-the-furrow,' said I. So," continued Bhagirathi coming forward, "Lord, she gave us this sign on our forehead. You can see it's the kumkum from her brows, our iris, the iris of her honey-vermillion hue."

The Lord was so touched. He laid his two thumbs on the two sides of the sparrows of Benares that whatever happens they would not be eaten by vultures or be killed by the hawk. These Rama-marks on the sparrows of the right have come generation after generation, and just as no crocodile will touch you when you bathe in Benares, no vulture will touch the Rama-sparrows. They seem, as it were, to have eyes on their wings. For at the moment when Rama laid his fingerprints on them Sri Rama had not broken the arc of Shiva nor he seen Sita Devi yet. But when he returned on his way to Ayodhya and with his new-wed Queen, the holy couple stopped and gave a few nuptial rice-grains to these sparrows so that they now eat only the virtuous grains of pilgrims. Thus after many lives they're born again as men, and sometimes even as brahmins. And why not I ask of you, a sparrow be born a brahmin? The wise Bhim the parrot says: Are you still there, O race of Bhagirathi? The brahmin is dead with his lucre as the English with their greed. In Benares we know no caste but virtue. "Oh, ho," says the vulture of the right, "and what about us then? You don't want us to be like those butchers on the other side eating of buffalo flesh?" Bhim turns to Rupvati and says, "Talk to them, I cannot. I must go on with my meditations."

The bharadwaj-bird now comes in poking her nose in every one's affairs, that eternal thief. The vultures, knowing the bharadwaj has not only a long tail but a long tongue, frighten her and say, "Don't you meddle in our affairs." "What," says the bharadwaj, "I am only a praying bird forever willing to eat off the leavings of pilgrims. What are you angry about?" The vultures do not argue, they hiss. It's then Rupvati says, "When my lord is in meditation we need no intruders. Will you just keep quiet?" Which explains why when the bells are ringing for evening worship, and, of a sudden the night falls, there's a long silence as if the temple water-tank were shaken by the breezes, and between the shake and the splash there's the space of no-sound. The wavelets by the Ganges play about as if in adoration of evening, and when the bells ring high, and the drums beat and the leaping pilgrims of the boat wash their hands and feet, and beat their cheeks seeking forgiveness, and they fold their hands in worship, on the neem tree there, there's a wide-awake silence. By the red-stone of Prabhavathi Devi a lamp has been lit. On all the verandas the lamps leap from house to house, and Benares begins its evening of worship. The birds do not move any more. There are no bats on the neem tree. Sometimes, however, so old is Bhim that in the Bindu House you can hear his snore. Did you know parrots snored like men? They do.

And just a few days ago, as anybody will tell you in Benares, Bhim took his usual evening bath in the Ganga and was never seen again. And since that was the evening of the death of Swami Siddheshwarji, the great blind saint, the story is that one saw the bird, yes, Bhim, as he was known to every sadhu, fall into the pyre and die. This is perhaps just a rumour. It is believed Bhim came every day to be fed by Siddheshwarji, and when he knew he was going to leave his body, he told the bird: I am going away, you know, the day after tomorrow. This explains why Bhim never ate for two days, never left his perch. And then Bhim disappeared from the world.

Now Rupvati sits in her austerities biding her time.

III

Chhota Munna Lal (or Madhobha, as he was called) was a quiet, young man of the busy lanes of Benares. Playful and shrewd, grave but kindly, people wondered how all this could go bundled in together. Was there not some dark hole, some secret in that big chest of his, behind that fat talisman on the left arm, or the two unequal moles of his face, or in the large, moonstone ring he wore — was there something that everybody in Benares did not know, for all Benares knew him — or had the great Shiva really made this young man as good as he looked? He always wore silk shirts, his collar neatly ironed, and a shy elegant scarf around it — his dhoti was ever well-creased, his tilak on the forehead was round and big (it was made of sandal paste and sanctuary butterlamp black) and he put on collyrium around his big bursting eyes. For he ever seemed to be going out on a hunt, and when asked he'd say, as if in jest: "I have a rendezvous with a lovely spirit — I see her only on moonlit nights. And she is so beautiful. All the beauties of this earth seem as nothing." "And with your profession?" you asked, as he sold firewood for cremation." Yes, sir, it's because of my profession that I can see spirits. You only see the dead. I see beyond the dead. Anyway my Mohini is not of the world of the dead. She is so real, not a dancing girl of Benares — and I have seen most of them — can match in beauty with this

Mohini." And you might see in the windows of the little attic he had, above the shop, small frills hanging, long threads of gold, garlands, and one heard of lovely earrings, naga head-jewels, fripperies, bangles, and they all lay, so people imaged, on a tray under a large gilt-framed looking glass. But how could anybody say anything, for nobody had gone into the room in the last five years, no, nobody. She would come, so once again the Benares legend ran, she would come through the mirror to pick her lover's gifts whensoever she wanted, and she came often. You knew of her presence because of the melody she sang — and she sang as no. humans sang:

sa ri ga sa ri ga sari ga.....
sa ri ga sa, sa ri ga, sari ga sa
sa ri pa ma ga sa, sa ri gamma ga
ma ga sa...etc.

She never sang a song but always notes. And you could slip into sleep and hear them, there, that was her mystery. And she sang to you all through the goodliest sleep, so said our Madhobha, whenever he was elated. Otherwise he spoke little.

"Ho, Madhobha." It was the boss calling. Benares has no night. The dead have no night. They die at all times, diurnal or nocturnal, and the firewood has to be kept ready. The fact is when the monsoon comes, and when it does come, it does come and pour oceans on Benares, you know, like a howling police inspector spitting and kicking and thundering, and then there's the rain of a thousand years. You understand, the firewood then can be disastrously wet. The boss does not care. "The less it burns," says he, "the more they'll buy." But the brahmins are keen masters in this choice of good firewood. Their tasks have to be finished quicker. Otherwise they would lose their next client. So between the brahmin and the firewood-sellers there was, as it were, an ancient pact: four annas to the rupee would go to the brahmins. That made firewood costlier for the dead. But then who will not pay dearer prices for the dead? You can ask a hundred thousand rupees, and if they could, they'll pay it to you. "Take it, brother, and give me the good firewood! Golden, goddess firewood!" Also, the price you fix will go with the face you see. You've learnt by now that a lean face is tricky, and the price should be medium (say, seven rupees eight annas a maund) and if he has a fat face you can be sure (were he even a bania) he has a big heart. Also you must be able to judge who's dead from the face of the customer: brother, mother, wife, or grandfather or a nobody of anybody. Somehow in Benares grandfathers fetch the highest prices. If you ask Madhobha why so, he says, does Madhobha, "Because the grandfathers have always the treasure-trunks with them." And they dote on their granddaughters. There is generally a widowed daughter or granddaughter to look after the grandfather. And she is usually very kind. So you can go up to eight rupees four annas a maund (and the brahmins get a slightly higher proportional sum). It's gay with the dead in Benares, you talk of them as you talk of tamarind or mangoes, or of trains. "Are you taking the Jaunpur Express?" is just like saying, "Sathu Madhurai is dead, and he will be brought to the ghats, in half an hour. The home-rites are almost over. The brahmins came just a while ago. They couldn't find a fourth. That's the delay. But now they'd have found one."

The fourth in Benares is the magical man. He's the highest paid of the shoulder-bearers. He is so difficult to find — sometimes a neighbour will say: "Come, I'll do it." And, brother, I tell you, such men are less rare in Benares than you think.

But, by the time Madhobha has come down from his attic — and he seems ever awake — the boss is already measuring down the plunge-weight firewood. It has been raining a steady big rain for a day and a half, and the water cleverly seeps even through the protective panels of the shed. Water is clear-minded, you know; anyway how can any one protect you from that bitch, the monsoon? "Is not that so, Panditji?"

Jamnalal is the name of the boss. Jamnalal Mothichand Bhabra is writ on the sign board hanging lamely at the gate. *Himalayan Firewood* in faded English characters. He lives with his three puling, snotty children on the groundfloor, and the yard is made of a low mangy mango tree. Underneath it come and lie the logs from Sonapur and Jaunpur, and from the Himalayan tarais. They have to be dried first and then chopped, splintered and sold. Firewood is so dear these days — war or no war, firewood is always dear. "Madhobha, that wretch has made havoc even with our new supply. Go and see in the backyard shed. You must give these good people dry firewood." "Sir merchant, please be so kind. Give us the driest wood you have." And Madhobha plays the game. He brings more firewood from the shed (you can see his moving lantern as he goes toward the backyard and the way he walks back, the lantern left behind) and he lays the firewood on the balance. The balance creaks for a sneeze or a stretch of arm, and would she not, the old witch, when you have added on maunds more of fat wet firewood? "We always keep special dry firewood for the good," says Jamnalal, and when one of his children waking, cries, he shouts: "Hé you son of a widow, can't you shut your mouth, even when the night is dense? Shut up, do you understand?" And you then hear is young wife strike the child. The child cries louder, for in monsoon time it's not so unpleasant to be beaten. Isn't that so? But, little by little, you begin to enjoy the strike more. Somehow you even like a firm hit better than a bad beating, and monsoon is good because you are thrashed well. It warms you. Which proves by the way, why the poor shivering uncle or granddaughter will pay eight rupees four annas for the rock-weight firewood, and then Madhobha will put it all on the hand-cart and push it down the Benares cobbles, for what are Benares streets but boulders broken fat, and round, and slippery, and when it rains, the wretch slips more. The dogs in Benares do not bark when you carry firewood — they know it's for the dead. They too would be dead one day, but there would, alas, be no firewood for them. Thus the common area of silence.

Either out of envy or of compassion the dogs of Benares come with you a short distance as you go toward the burning ghat. And the fact is they know the nature and the smells of each brahmin — they know whom to tease, and whom to smell from a distance, and whom to insult with a long unconvincing bark. They have such knowledge too (the dogs have) of the true nature of the dead: good or mischievous, cheat or saintly, they can say from the son or disciple who walks in front with the ember-pot. The Benares curs can tell a saintly dead from a hundred yards. There's still a story current in Benares. When Sadhu Shivarajji died not long ago, all the curs on Dashashwamedh Ghat stood by the pyre silent as if they were old, old friends. They spent the whole night there, seated on their backsides, and one or two of them even growled as the pyre began to die out. These are facts, and if you care to know you have only to ask Madhobha; he is well informed on all that happens on the Benares ghats, below, above and even in between, because of his Mohini.

By the time you've pushed your cart to the ghats and Jamnalal has pushed his, and you rest them against the parapet wall, the firewood has still to be carried down to the cremation ground. The cremation ground is not always free. How could it be? Somebody else is being burnt too and so you edge your way to a side, and heap up your own firewood. The Doms[1] now take charge of it. It's their heaven-ordained right. And as you well know, in Benares only the heavens rule.

The body has not yet come, and this makes Madhobha shiver, for the air is still wet. He sits on the ghats looking

---

1. Families for thousands of years, so it is said, have inherited these privileges.

at Mother Ganga and telling her noble things while the Doms are now busy with their fiery job. For Madhobha, Ganga is the real Mother and Mohini her daughter. "Gangaji," says Madhobha, "do be kind to me. You know I never pray — I just forget to pray. You know I have no time to come and bathe in you often. I sit under a tap, by the shop, and have a quick shower. But all water is Ganga water. Gangaji, you know my heart is all with you. I worship you, Mother, as a calf worships its cow."

And when the dead comes — and you can hear it all a league away because of the conches or the chants or the sobbing men — you say "and now to the job." Madhobha knows exactly where to lay the firewood and helps the Dom about so that it does good work. For example the sprintly ones have to be on a side so that the wind might carry the fire over to the centre. The big ones have to be in the middle, otherwise they will never get dry. The art of arranging firewood for a pyre is a complicated business. The Doms got it from Shiva himself, Lord of the crematorium, but they are so degenerate now. Where the head is going to lie you must have light small pieces. The head is the most difficult human complement to burst open. And if you've some sandalwood it is their proper place to be laid faithfully. Sandalwood is heavy but burns well emitting much heat. However, what you must not do is lay big logs on a side. They never never take on, and the relatives of the dead will curse you, and when they come back for more firewood, they have all your own dead ancestors on their tongue for abuse. It's an honest business, you know, in Benares to sell firewood. But you must not be soft. You must know people are always dying in the world. Do not the Puranas say there is one man dying at every eye-wink of the world, and at least for ten eye-winks of Benares, is there a man ready for the funeral. All the dead are not good. This much you learn too from the trade. For if he's an evil man you know he will need more firewood than any others, and the brahmins knowing all this will not wait for him till he's all burnt to pure ash (unless he is sort of a lakhpathi). The fact is the good burn quickly. Ask those people at the University to explain this, with their well-printed English texts? And look at the faces of the dead. Most of them are so peaceful. They do not even seem asleep, they seem to be talking gently to themselves. Sometimes one wonders whether the curs of Benares do not understand their talk. For suddenly a cur begins to whine. "What is it you are saying, Kala?"

There's one type of the dead Madhobha does not like. He hates the young dead. For him this is totally wrong. Something went wrong somewhere, that any young man or woman could die. "What did he die of, mother?" — "Tuberculosis?" — "And your child, what it did die of, father?" — "Of hiccups." — " And you, grandfather, what is it your granddaughter died of?" — " Of sorrow." She lost her husband. They had been married for two years. And on the same day as her husband, today, she dies. ("I want to join him. I want to join him," she said.) "She will join him, grandfather." And when Madhobha goes home and talks to his Mohini on the other side, he says, "Protect her, beloved, this lady on her journey. She loved her husband so!"

Madhobha of course is not sentimental. Tears come to him with difficulty. You must see him when he goes to the wrestling matches. He can down an adversary in three slippery movements, and, there, look he's seated on the chest of his adversary. He likes wrestling for it makes him feel he's strong, and not a good for nothing rascal. At home in the village (when his mother was alive) they said: Modhi, he's like a hen, all ashiver for every cough or sneeze. So, one early morning, he went to the Hanuman temple, and vowed he would get strong. Then he went and fell at the feet of Sadanand, the Zamindar's cook, who knew wrestling. "Teach me wrestling, and I'll give you two rupees." — "You come on a Saturday at the Maruthy temple, and bring coconut and flowers and we'll perform puja and I'll give you your first lesson." The first lesson was splendid and in two years he, growing into a young man of sixteen, beat his own brahmin teacher. And soon he lost his father and then his mother — he was only nineteen. An elder brother is no father or mother. "There's always Mother Ganga for the orphan," he said, and came to the holy city of Benares. He found no difficulty in finding a job: he looked so strong, he could lift a mountain. And in Benares there aren't such hefty people anymore. "Except on Saturday," said Madhobha, to the boss. "On that day I go to the Hanuman temple for worship, and maybe wrestle a little." — "We don't want a wrestler here. We're happy if you are a man." "I can lift a one-maund log like a flower," he said, did Madhobha, and lifted a big log in such a playful manner, Jamnalal engaged him on the moment. Ultimately it costs you less to have a strong man. The weak take a cycle of years to make a single trip to the shed and back, and in monsoon time they need help to push the hand-carts to the ghats. And the children so loved Madhobha.

Jamnalal soon discovered Madhobha never never went to women. This again makes things simple. The other fellow Paltoo, who was there, not long ago, was always eyeing women, and never looked at his firewood, even once, decently. And women, I tell you, are the bane of Benares. There are too many of them and most of them seem to have but one job. Even the rich widows who come, they are not without casting eyes on a young male pushing his firewood cart to the ghats. Virtue does not grow easily in Benares. And vice has no better place. For all comes here to burn. "Shambho, Shankara."

Madhobha does not believe he's virtuous. He just obeys what he'd learnt. On Saturdays he sort of fasts in the morning, and goes on to the Maruthi temple during the early afternoon. When he's said the name of Ram a thousand and eight times, and has rung the bell, and offered his flowers, and the camphor is lit, he pays his fee to the brahimns, and prasad in hand he goes to Chhotelal for some puris. Chhotelal's puris are famous all over Benares — he makes them with some special flour from Jaunpur, and they are transparent as is muslin. And Chhotelal's chutneys are famous, they'd be remembered in heaven. Madhobha then drinks a large glass of milk — hot milk with a layer of fat cream on it. From there he goes to the wrestling centre and he plays about with anyone there. Most of them fear his tricks but they like him because whether defeated or winning he always laughs. He rarely bets on any wrestler. He thinks money is precious, and it will one day serve a good purpose. At some wrestling matches the agents have paid him as much as two hundred rupees. He puts it all in his steel pot and buries it under the mango tree, deep under the pile of firewood. Nobody knows it, not even the ants. And that explains why he always asks for silver coins from customers and refuses to take paper notes. How much money he has there he does not know. People say he keeps all the money for his marriage. This is not true. For he will never marry. The brahmin cook of the Zamindar had said: "There's strength in your limbs — and Bhakta Hanuman gives it to you — because there's virility in you loins. As long as like Hanuman you're a brahmachari, you will be a splendid wrestler — that is if the Lord willeth. Rama — Rama, Hé Raghupathi. May He protect you."

Madhobha loves his wrestling more than he would any woman. What would he do with women anyway — those puling, plundering, slavish looking maternal lionesses, you bow to them from afar, but never go near them. And as for the rest you have Devi Annapurna, the benign goddess in her lovely temple, there by her Lord Vishwanath!

But now he has the Mohini. One day some three years or so ago, when Madhobha was sitting in his attic, he heard the sound of anklets and bangles, and he knew a woman was near. And before he could know who, a melody arose more gracious than of any human tongue, and a lit loveliness danced before him as never man hath seen.

He sat in rapt devotion to this feminine presence as if more than a goddess were there — a woman too was there. And she threw flowers at him and real flowers too they were, for he gathered them and stuck some behind his ears, for every time there was a visitation she clapped her hands and danced. Loveliness was the wrong word for her. It was, Madhobha used to tell himself, something like light seen reflected in a holy pond — it becomes more beautiful, as oil lamps on a Ganges evening. She spoke softly and called him by his name! "Madhobha," she said, "I love you and may I come to visit you sometimes? I like the way you worship your God Hanuman. I see you often on your way to the temple. One day when I sat at dusk on the parapet of a terrace, and there was absolute noiselessness, I heard a strange sound as if Sri Rama was going back to Ayodhya, such the pleasant splendid noise of horses and elephants. I looked down and it was you. I followed you to the temple. I saw Ramji himself standing behind Hanuman to bless you. I have lived so long looking for some one who could take me to Ram. For we're of such stuff made, we cannot approach a god directly. We have to go through a man. And a man who has never touched a woman is our man. You are that — one can see from the curls of your eyebrows. We can smell it in the smells of your skin, at the pores of your hair, we, and our sisters." She spoke so simply, did the Mohini, and her song was so deep divine. Yes, that is the true word!

Madho swore allegiance to her and worshipped her in his heart. What need of a woman more worthy than a Mohini? You know they do exist. Shop-keeper Pannalal in Kanpur had a second son who had seen a Mohini. So had he, Bulla, the madcap. They say he went mad, because a Mohini had captured his heart. It's better to be mad with a Mohini than live with a human shrew. Life is so easy: You bathe and you sell firewood, you eat (the food gets almost cooked by itself, when you have such fine firewood at home) and you sleep, and when the little one of Bapulal (the neighbour vegetable seller) comes, or the cur called Sunder from Dashashwamedh Ghat, you play with them. Mahmud the son of Ustad Rahman Khan, the musician, sometimes comes too and talks to Madho of his father. Madho has heard the great music of the Ustad. It was so like the Mohini's but hers is better because when she sings, you see sound flying. You see the colour of every raga. She sings usually in Kalyani but she has no words for her song. It's as I told you, always *sarigapada'sa*. When does she come? She comes whenever she wants to really, but preferably on full moon nights. She likes her jewels to shine and her hair to rise and fall to a rhythm. Madho never knows when she's left. He wakes up:

"Hé, is there anybody there?"

"Yes, sethji. I am coming down."

"What do you charge for your firewood?"

"Ten eight a maund."

"Go and tell it to the trees."

"Let us make it ten, then."

"Do you think me such an idiot?"

"You can take a round of Benares, and come back. You will always come to us. We sell the best firewood. And we sell it cheapest." By now you are face to face with your buyer.

"And how much do you want, of sandalwood?"

"Just plain firewood is what we want. We are not maharajas. Make it six rupees and four annas." The customer is touching the firewood to see if it's dry.

"What are they?"

"The tarai teak. Boy or man?"

"Boy of fourteen. Died of dysentery."

"I'll make it eight rupees, for it's a mere boy."

"Six-eight and not a pice more." As he tries to go out Jamnalal had woken up. His children were already up and crying. He gave them few shouts and then he came out.

"He seems a good man. Make it seven-eight, Madho."

"You're a nice boss," says Madho. "Do you want to sell

your goods for less than you bought them with? And how long will you run your shop, boss?"

Nevertheless the bargain is made. Seven rupees is what it will be. When Madhobha felt he liked someone (whose body he wanted to see) all the curs knew that the dead was a good person. And the curs will come in procession behind Madhobha because it's a good soul that's dead. And when the pyre is lit, this time all the curs bark. There's more mystery in the world than you know. In Kalabhairav's temple, sometimes you can see monkeys, devotees of Hanuman come. Between the dog and monkey there's marriage in Benares. Madho has a great following among the dogs and the monkeys because he worships Hanuman. "Hé Rama. Raghu Rama. Sita Rama."

Sometimes Madho likes to sit by the pyre and weep with the dead's relations. "Ho Ho Ho," he cries and says: "What shall I do without you, son?" as if the dead were made of his. He likes people. He will do anything for anybody. But just don't shout up when he's seeing his Mohini. Then he becomes so fierce he can tear a porcupine to his very skin. Once, he almost tore his boss into a million bits. "Get out, you slave, you pig. Or I'll hang your skin on the ghats for the vultures." The next morning he remembers nothing. Did he really shout back that? "Oh Shiva-Shiva, forgive the sinner." Then he recognises the flowers behind his ears, and remembers.

"Oh father," he says to his boss, "forgive this heavy sleeper."

"But you looked so awake?"

"Did I? I must have been dreaming."

"You were so frightening. I thought you would do what you said."

Madhobha fell on his boss's feet and beat his cheeks and begged pardon, and went to serve the new customer. There's always work in Benares. And it pays.

IV

Muthradas of Vrindavan[1] sold his camels, and came to die in Benares. His family had always traded with Kathiawar and West Rajasthan selling beads and bangles (some of these made in Benares — of wax and broken mirrors — and that's how Muthradas first came to Benares, as a boy of eleven. (but this was so long ago, when the sepoy mutiny was still remembered by the elders, and the good Victoria Queen had taken over her big empire to rule and decided to give it a just administration) and they also sold, did the Kanakmal's family, winter blankets and cheap Kanpur prints for the peasant women. They naturally traded in kumkum and turmeric ("and fresh from Benares ghats" would always be added on for the benefit of each customer); but what Muthradas enjoyed most when still a boy was the autumnal deserts (on his way to Jaisalmer, Bhuj or Amber) when the rain-grass had not yet disappeared and birds were still with the young. Muthradas would suddenly wake to an auspicious dawn — as if all of Lord Krishna's cattle had been awakened by the flute (as the tradition says), and they tugging at their tethers to rush to him, the milk-maids behind them and the cowherds behind them again — you could hear the long drawn *amme, amme,* of the matronly cows (those who'd

---

1. Famous for its association with Sri Krishna.

had eight and nine calves, and their udders touched their knees) and the narrow shrill low of the young calves. But when you looked round you only saw the peacocks pecking at their grains under the babul trees, and far away other camels with other Mohammeds leading the caravan.

Mohammed was a tall old Muslim from Ajmer, and for him, his beads and his Friday prayers meant more than all the treasures you could give him — and his loyalty to his masters came next only to his knee-bent prayer. He and his fathers had served generations of this Kanakmal's family, and some Kanakmals had even given them land (this lay some two miles off the Agra road where the Jamuna suddenly makes a bend and turns on herself before going towards Bori Ghat) and you could see, if you so wished, all the eight or nine camels of the Kanakmal's buried there one after the other with Muradabadi incense holders, Ajmeri bier-cloth, and all, and it brought such brightness to the countryside. The fact of the fact is, what makes truth makes joy. What could make truth better than an ancient loyalty? "Salt is silver when the tongue is lord," thus goes a saying. If you've eaten of Kanakmal's salt, generation after generation, to be loyal to them is like asking the feet to obey the head, is it not so, sir, dear sir? Remember life is only a caravan, as the saying goes: Does one know what a fresh dawn would bring, once the desert night is over?

For Muthradas the dawns of the Mewar deserts were as precious as gifted kingdoms — he revelled in their intrepid beauty. He sometimes thought of his wife Lakshmi too. They had been married for four years now — it was all vague and incoherent — but he could still recollect the music, and the elephant ride. Lakshmi was a bright girl, six years of age, and from a luminescent family — they had many hangings of brocade in their houses, and many hookas in their reception halls, with embroidered white wall-pillows. But plague and cholera came, and one by one it took away one member of the family after the other, and as you know, such calamities did happen in those days —

while one pillar after the other, as it were, fell, only an elder aunt, a sister and the big step-brother remained. Word came that Lakshmi was all the time weeping, sitting under a ladder and counting her days. She wanted to go to the home of her lord and husband. But what could Muthradas do? He was too small, and after all a woman comes to the house only when your moustache has stuck up the lip. Muthradas scratched his chin and found it smooth. A wife meant something to that little thing between the legs, but that hallowed night was far, far away. One becomes a man (and has children all all that) when one is grown up. At eleven years of age, you take summer lesson from the Munshi in reading and accounting and ride with uncle Ramchand to Kathiawar for the autumn sales. And you came back long before Shivaratri — though sometimes you went to Benares instead, for the festival, and bought mirrors and things for the marriage season. Thus life.

The Rajasthani peacocks are an eyeful to gaze at — they are magical when they touch each other by the beak. Sometimes a cheetah cub has been left behind, and the village is all gathered round this lost orphan Why could the villagers not see, thought Muthradas, that it weeps — it weeps like Lakshmi does, perhaps. Would they have a pet cheetah when they have a larger house, in Vrindavan? No, for the cheetah eats meat, and no decent person ever eats meat, except, the low class people, and the Europeans, who also eat the pig, so the elders say. However Mohammed does not eat the pig. But then Mohammed is not of this world. He has all those ancestors buried on his field, near where their camels lie, and he is all of them made into one thought. And then he is ever in prayer. Those who pray are good, so Mohammed is good. Therefore, it is he who does not eat meat, though he eats mutton but no beef. Which makes it simple why Mohammed must go and get Lakshmi to the house.

The truth is nobody gets you your wife except the stars. Try as you might and make every scheme to go and see her (after all you could go to Sawai Madhopur where her family lived) and as it were, lose your way with the camels, and, so to say, find yourself at Lakshmi's door. But Lakshmi is not so easy to see, she's always in the ladies' quarters. Mohammed could take a message — a ring from Muthradas like Hanuman took the signet ring of Sri Rama for Sita, when she was prisoner of that ogre Ravana. "This, the signet ring, that the Lord of the Raghu race, in love for the fair recognition of Sita, sendeth, etc., etc." No, this could never be. Look, look, the caravan is getting lost in the morning haze. Camels are eaten up by nothingness, and what remains behind are but Abdul Kader and Shamshir, the three camels, and the sound of their bells. Lord, it's good to lie awake on a moving camel, and dream of Lakshmi.

It took three more years for Lakshmi to "come home," and it was so big-like to be truly married. You entered your apartments, and awaited Lakshmi. After every piece of housework was finished, Lakshmi would slip in, and ever so shyly, with a silver tumbler of milk. The excited pleasure you get, after it all, to whom can you say? To no one. Lakshmi simply wept, she wept, that she was rid of her step-brother and all. Here, in this largesome house, it was great to be the eldest son's wife. The mother-in-law was not always nice, true! But often she fed you with milk-cream after every shout: Poor orphan, she would say. And so the world moved on its hinges — circular and clear, and at night the milk, the shyness, and all the implicate bounty of limb and lip. Life is beautiful when you go with the whole family to Radha Mata temple, in the evening, and tell the goddess what you cannot say to any one. "Mother, happiness is marriage. Mother, give me a baby boy soon, soon." She did not know then — she was so young — no Kanakmal can have a son, but by adoption. It was a curse uttered by a Kanakmal wife, one Anusuya-ben — over a hundred years ago, as she drowned herself slowly in the Jamuna, one winter dawn, for her husband's betrayal with a concubine. And she was a Pativrata, and who does not know such a curse will last for at least seven generations? It is a fact as real as the Jamuna flow towards Prayag to join the Ganga, and together they flow as Maha-Ganga to holy Benares. Thus the truth.

Muthradas and Lakshmi-ben were married for just fifty years. Nobody in the family now remained, uncles and aunts they died one after the other with this illness or that or of old age, which comes whether you want it or not — while the Kathiawar autumn festivals' demands became less with Ahmedabad millware, and the Kanakmal's family had only the old couple left, their account books, and many, many pillars. And just three camels. Muthradas adopted his second cousin's son Moti Chand (a boy of seven), and before he could finish even his high school he showed up his ancestry. Through his mother he was connected with the Raghav Das Nathumals of Palitana. Now you understand!

He made unnecessary demands, and asked for monies and monies again, and was found, one morning, in the gutter by a prostitute's house. They married him off but that brought no help. He beat his wife and eloped with a brahmin pilgrim to Delhi. One wept at home, and one asked astrologers. "In three years Rahu's position in the third house will be free, and he will return — do not fear." Indeed just as the astrologer had predicted, after three years Moti appeared, neat and simple, as if much had happened within these intervening years. He stayed a model husband (life sometimes plays those awful tricks of Rahu or Ketu, it does not matter) and then he too died childless leaving behind his widow. Vrindavan was all sorrow and tears for Muthradas and Lakshmi-ben. But one day, a few months later, Lakshmi-ben herself was killed by a bus as she was crossing the street, after feeding the cows at the Goshala opposite (Oh these New Delhi bus drivers). Muthradas had no heart even for Vrindavan anymore — he left his daughter-in-law and her adopted son (he seemed a bright child and a good grandson who'd offer the annual funeral feast to his departed ancestors) and Muthradas with his cloth bundle, his Ramayana, and his small cash, came to Benares and settled there forever.

His room on the third floor of Ananda Mahal building had always light at night — he read philosophical books. In the afternoons, however, he went to hear the Ramayana — Pandit Uday Shankerji of Kalyan gave ecstatic discourses on Tulsi Ramayana and hardly had he wiped his tears, then he came back home, ate his dry rice and pickle, and opened his books of philosophy. Vedanta is a heady subject and if you're not aware, you will fall into unsuspected pits. He searched for a Guru, did Muthradas, and found one by the Ambasamudram hospice. The Guru was a man from the South but spoke some Hindi (he could speak English too, but Muthradas knew no English). The Guru's sacred name was Sankarananda. Muthradas was given his initiation after some three years of spiritual practices. Many problems in Vedanta are connected with dream and sleep. They became a little clearer now. Muthradas had always believed you slept when you slept and you dreamt when you dreamt. What meaning could they have? But in Vedanta there's so much talk of the waking state, the dream, dreamer and so on. And the nature of deep sleep is beyond comprehension. "Seeing, hearing, thinking and knowing are always experienced by people in dream, moreover, as they are essentially the Self. It is directly known." Sitting by the lamplight (electricity, though available, seemed a luxury), he read his Sri Sankara. The hurricane lantern helped you at night in your room, and at dawn it followed you to the ghats for your lavations. Shambho Shankara. Muthradas opened his Upadesha Sahasriyam and read again. "There is no vision in me as I am without the organ of seeing. How can there be hearing for me who have no auditive organ? Devoid of the organ of speech I have no action of speaking in me. How can there be thinking in me who have no mind?"

He waits for death, does Muthradas, as one waits for a car, the car that will take you to the Railway Station. "Grandfather, don't you worry, you'll catch the Agra Express. It arrives only at eleven-nineteen. It's only nine-thirty now." But then there's all the town to cross — sometimes you're held up at the market square, or by the Boli Chawl Mosque, were it a Friday morning. A cur might run under your wheel or the engine may suddenly go phut. What a procession life is till you get to the station. The fact is, the Agra Express is always on time (even after Indian Independence). If death does not know time, pray who does? Time, however, is so evasive with man.

Muthradas gets three letters a year from his adopted grandson. The grandson writes for his father's funeral-anniversary and for his adopted grandmother's obsequies ("the brahmins were well pleased, and so must the manes have been, for such the auspicious caw-cawings of the crows after the feast"). He writes again on the eighth day of Dusshera, and finally on the first day of Divali, before he opens his new account book. The Kathiawar market has since been made up partially with touristic demands, today you have pilgrims and tourists. There are no camels now, and so no Mohammed. It's all a past story. But when the trains rumble on the Dufferin Bridge you wonder if you should not put on your clothes and go down for the car. One should never make the car wait. For once you go you never come back. It's just a question of courtesy.

Before the third letter of the year, this year (that is 1963) the car was at the door, and the four-shoulder brahmins took his last procession to the ghats. Muthradas' skull splits in no time — he was a virtuous man, of this there was no doubt. He had not yet discovered the true similarity between the waking state and the dream state, but there are still so many life cycles to come. Man goes where he has to go but one day he will arrive where there's no going or returning. A car can always take you to the railway station. But you don't need (or do you?) a car to go to yourself? No.

V

"Bhedia! Bhedia!" you say, as he grins, "Bhedia, how did you ever come here?" and he smiles with his broad hands, he makes signs with his nose (lifting it back and forth, and then hiding his face between the knees), he answers, does Bhedia, "The cucumber was bad so it became sad. The cucumber was bad so it became sad." "Now what does that mean?" you may ask Bhedia, and he replies as if it were clear as his eyes (and he had beautiful dark eyes, with rounded eyebrows, long eyelashes and a limpid wheat-coloured skin under)'. "The moon went up to the sky and stood, and the hill suddenly became a lake so that Ramji and Krishnaji could besport themselves in Vrindavan, you understand!" And Bhedia takes a long gasp of breath, with his hookah. "So Benares became a hotel.[1] You understand — you buy and you sell. You sell puri and halva, and cowries for gold, and all the monkeys make marriages. All the marriages in this city are made by monkeys," affirms Bhedia with a look of friendly contempt. "First Arjun came to the forest and got caught in the house of wax and that was in Benares. Now, Rama lost his sheep, and the donkeys went astray. You know donkeys like those who graze on the Ganges banks. And I came

---

1. Both a cafe and a restaurant are called hotels.

here, the noble son of Kunti, and that was long ago. Long after the Mahabharata was,"[2] says Bhedia and laughs into his things. "Life is so funny, Maharaj. Before the war I served a Prince. He was so kind, and he had four black horses. I groomed them and fed them and harnessed them, and crying, 'Hé, Hé, the prince of Chandrapur!' I took him about town in his large, spacious landau, made in London you understand, yes, in London, and drove him to the railway station, to the mills, to the club, to his mistresses. Oh, to be sure he had a concubine and a good one at that. She always had jellebies and sent them to me through the backyard — she knew I loved sweets. I gave them all to the horses. My horses were like Nala's, they could span the skies in an hour, and be in Indra's kingdom in a day. In my own time I have seen many a swayamvara ceremony. I was at Bhoja Raja's swayamvara and at that of Vikramaditya's daughters. I was wherever there was duty to perform," and here suddenly Bhedia burst into tears, and the pilgrims who stood by the Ganges banks, prasad in their hands and hair, would look at Bhedia, his woebegone tatters, his idiotic smile, his long nails and his unwashed presence, and would turn away and look at the Ganges to feel pure and safe.

But Bhedia was, if you want to know, one of the great men in Benares. He never scorned. He never spat on anyone. He felt he was a saint. "Why sir," he would say, "in the kingdom of Indra deep in Heaven," and he would point at the sky, "there's a lake called the lake of Vishada. There, there are many mermaids and each one more beautiful than the other. I used to go up there betimes when my master slept in the afternoon: mills and back, and drink, and lunch. And thus," Bhedia would show the palm of his hand, and lay his head on it, "Master Krishna Prakash used to sleep up till three or four. Meanwhile I would whisk the flies off my horses and take a trip to

---

2. Bhedia here confused the heroes of the Mahabharata and the Ramayana.

Indra's Kingdom. The difference between the two is simple. Here train runs, there cities move. You don't go to a city. The city comes to you. You think, and it is there! 'Palace,' you shout and you are in a bright lit palace, with marble halls — and, what shall I say, even woman guards, and fierce cockfights. What's the use of a palace without a cockfight? Once upon a time I used to own cocks and fought them till they bled. One of them, Chilla, was like a buffoon. He played tricks with every one, and when he struck it was like a thunderbolt, it killed every other cock. That's why I am so happy in Benares, do you hear, sir? The river goes where it willeth, the crows caw, they caw, caw! Dancing girls become saints in this city, Maharajas wash the feet of Sadhus, and your Bhedia is here because one day his master got so angry. 'Hé, you idiot,' he cried from the porch of the bungalow (and that was in Lucknow, and he was a rich man and a big man), 'hé, Bhedia you idiot, and you haven't even learnt to make my bedding roll, you a thousand times idiot, a million times idiot!' and sir, he gave me such a kick, here, just on my man's big little tidbit, I just rolled and rolled on the floor squealing like a panicked cur, and praying to Shivji: 'Take me away, Lord, and make me anything but make me a good servant.' A good servant sir," and here Bhedia adds some more chillum into his smoke, "a good servant is like a good swing. It knows exactly where to go and when to come. A good servant is like nobody. A good servant is like a big jackfruit, like a saint, like a wide-eared elephant. It's no use being a bad servant, sir, it's unpleasing unto God. God did not make man to be bad, it is like a monkey that apes man. Better be a monkey, I said to myself, sir, and came to the holy city of Benares. But I cannot climb trees. I can steal fruits all right," and here from the folds of his dhoti Bhedia would produce all sorts of curious finds: dirty newspapers, beedies, sacred threads, nails, toothbrush of neem-twigs — he would produce babies' caps, a woman's choli-piece with lovely peacock designs, mango-stones, a gold ring, and some squashed coconut bits, two buttons, and an orange. "Hé," he giggled, "don't you think I steal better than they?" and he looked up and laughed at the monkeys. "Life is easier for me than for them. I hate calling them by their real name. They understand man's language and one day or the other they take revenge. So I was saying, I am a man, therefore, I walk on foot. They have to crawl on all their limbs. A man trusts man. A man does not trust a four-legged thief. Two legs are right. And you steal and you run just like this. Hé," and he shouts. But the whole lane laughs. Who does not know Bhedia, our younger brother? So noble, so heart-clean, friend to all creatures and stones, and look here, he takes a stone out of his pocket and throws it at the dustbin crows, and — "and — and," he could find no words, so Bhedia looks up at you and laughs.

He is so lovable, is Bhedia, you would have to create him like Brahma himself if he did not be. For him all things are so real, so simple, and he can play a cat against the moon and the earth against Indra's kingdom, and yet he would not harm a chameleon. Chameleons change colour and so are evil. That's why muslims kill them — he, the brute, the betrayer. For Bhedia there is no betrayal. In Benares all is right. Shivji in the temple will make him a good servant, one day. The fact is, there is no sadhu however full of ire and tong-tonguing who does not pat him on the back "Hé Bhedia what's the news from Heaven?" they ask. "It's cold," shouts Bhedia turning on himself with chill shivering. "The sun has forgotten Indra's Heaven. And so it is chill like on the snows. When you have too much cold," says Bhedia, "you become like the Man of the Snows." Some eager Europeans even come to Bhedia led by an over-eager guide. "This man, sir, has seen seven Snow Men. He comes from their country. How are they, Bhedia?" Bhedia answers something in Hindi, and the guide gives the apt answers. "The Snow Men are tall. They are all white like the Europeans. The Snow Man eats only snow. One was even seen mating on the lake sides. The little ones are already big as a pony, etc." The Benares guides have such greed and a great imagination. I tell you, you cannot live in Benares if you have no imagination which explains why Bhedia is so happy here. For him the world is imaginationings. To live in one's imagination is truly to live in heaven, has said some village vulgar singer, has he not? But that's the truth of the matter. There is no better representative of man than Bhedia. Unless you think of Shalwar Khan.

Now Shalwar Khan, also a friend of Bhedia's, is just a different type of horse — it has five legs. You must understand what Bhedia means by this. A four-legged horse runs just like that, like those tied to an ekka. But with Shalwar Khan they run in any direction you like: back or forth. They can go forward going backwards or go upwards going downwards. For Shalwar Khan can grow mangoes where there's only a foot-high plant, he can play magic with his cobra, his loved one, his beloved one, his noble friend, his destiny, his God's companion; he can make his son Putli dance on earth, and then high up in heaven. Shalwar Khan can lay his travelling bundle under a neem or tamarind tree, spread his cloth at any cross-lane, and then plant his magic-pole into the earth, shake his drum-drum, and all the neighbourhood is suddenly awake: the children, as if woken from a dream, come lisping and tumbling, holding their aunt's hands, their maid's fingers, and the boys make a huge circle for the marvels to see. Putli loves to be a hero among boys, Putli's mother was forgotten on some river bank — she loved drink too much, and loved ghosts more than man, and Shalwar Khan's gods hated ghosts. So he abandoned his wife one day and ran off with Putli — he got into a train — his huge travelling bundle, his snake basket, and his oboe, and was he not successful in the train? Though at every other station he was thrown out by the ticket-collector, he and his son Putli, then four years old. Finally he came to Shiva's mighty city (Shalwar Khan's gods had some minor links with Shiva's minions — did they not?) and once you come to Benares how can you ever leave it? Tell me.

"Hé, bolo," he would start, and all the housewives would lean over the windows, with their washings, their ladles, or their combs in hand, they too would watch the show while the children are already down by the tamarind tree. "In the time of Rama," Shalwar Khan would start shaking his drum and say, "there was a cow and her name was Ma-Moo." "Yes, Ma-Moo," repeats Putli. "And Ma-Moo was always of bad temper, like a shrew." "Like a shrew," repeats Putli. "Give me my shrew." And now Shalwar Khan takes out his oboe, and as he begins to play over the serpent-box he says: "Hé Lord, you must rise, and adorn our court. What do you say to that?"

"Hé, Lord, I am here," says Putli, to the cobra whose hiss is now heard all around. And Bhedia who's joined the crowd says: "O, children, take care, go away, and stand at a distance, the great King of Serpents is there. Take care, his skin is gold, his eyes diamond, and his heart is that of a saint." "Of a saint," says Putli as if all these were known forever. "He, Bhedia," shouts Shalwar, "Come and sit with me here, and help me. You can lift the lid so that the great Prince may appear." Bhedia without a shake of fear goes straight and lifts the box-lid off, and there is our beautiful Naga, Lord, King, spreading his hood, and playful as play. He slips and whirls, quivering out his tongue with thirst as though music is what he lives on. Bhedia goes round and round the box whispering something to himself, fully fascinated. And then Putli tells the story.

"Once the Prince of Oudh came to his court." "To his court," repeats Bhedia. And fingers in their mouth the children are in rapt attention. Only the one-year-olds on the waists of their ayas are in tears. "O take me home. O take me home." "I'll give you honey, baby, I'll give you a piece of gold," sings Bhedia, and the babies become silent. The quiet Ganga flows. The dippers are dipping, the crows are cawing. The vultures vociferate from high pipal tops. On terraces the wet clothes of pilgrims hang with assiduity. The more the sun, the more holy would they be. The bazaars seem of a sudden silent — it's noontime and people like to eat and rest. Shalwar Khan now pushes the Naga's head down with the oboe and fixes back the lid of the serpent-box. And then drags out a bamboo-basket from his large cloth-sack. Putli will still come out from some terrace, boys, having disappeared before you, into the earth. Life is so like an oboe song.

"Ready, jump in," orders Shalwar Khan. Putli turns round and round on himself, greeting the spectators with folded hands.

Now suddenly he flops into the bamboo-basket and stretches himself flat, while Shalwar Khan carefully draws the lid on top, and covers it all with a red mango-leaf design muslin cloth. Shalwar Khan then swings his hand thrice round and round the box muttering a secret something to himself, and shouts: And then there is absolute silence as if the world has disappeared. "Hé, my son, Putli, my son, Putli, go to heaven and come. Do you hear, go to Indra's kingdom and return." "And return," murmurs Bhedia, sobbing, sobbing.

"Bhedia," shouts Shalwar Khan, "Bhedia, throw up the cloth. Tear open the lid." Bhedia does what he is told, for life after life, as you will know, he was only born to lift the lid off the magical basket. "And now, ye genteel folk of Benares, ye, men and women, search where you will, and you will find there is no Putli anywhere. He's gone, he's gone. The basket is empty. Look, kick at it and see. Here, I thrust this shimmering sword into it and see. Where is Putli gone? There's no Putli. In the kingdom of Rama, when Dasaratha had sent his son away in exile, people wept and said: Oh where have you gone, O son," relates Shalwar Khan, standing up and swinging his drum. "O son," says Bhedia, as if he knew exactly the meaning of the story, and had rehearsed it. " 'O father', says the holy son, 'I am gone nowhere. Let Bharathji, my ever-devout brother, rule in my place. But if you want to see me, just do one thing — call me, and I'll come from any tree, any terrace.' 'Come, my son,' says Dasarathji, I want so much to see you, I cannot sleep without a vision of your holy presence'". "Presence, O Revered Father and King, and here I come," shouts Putli from that high terrace, there beyond the tamarind tree. How did he get there? Under the earth and up into the sky? The children are wonderstruck. Yes, Putli went under the earth and came out of heaven, there! "Yes, Putli is a bright boy," says Shalwar Khan, lifting the lid off the snake-box. "Is he not, Hé, My Lord Naga, Lord of Dharma?" The Naga Lord hisses and plays with the music as if heaven and earth were indeed of one matter made, and Bhedia and Putli were of course denizens of a true and higher world. "Why, Benares is all like that," auntie said, when she took little Girija home.

Girija has come from Kashmir for the Ram Lila. It's wonderful to travel by bus and train, and be in Benares as if you were always there. Girija, who's now five years old, has been three months in Benares. He loves Benares because here children play. They play in gangs. For example, between house and house there are established links, and newcomers are immediately taken into the fold. There are no stranger in Benares. The king of the young is one Mohendra. Mohone, as they call him, is a good big boy, you think because he tends cows. That's not the truth at all, as any boy on Dashashwamedha Ghat will tell you. Mohendra and his gang are interested in teasing Sadhus, in thieving mangoes from shops, stealing clothes from bathers, and cigarettes from men's pockets. And money from anywhere. Mohendra and his gang are well set, and have a code of honour. You have to eat Mohone's spittle three times, and you're joined on to the fold. Mohone is eleven but he looks fifteen. His gang has some twenty persons unless you count Bhedia as one of them. If you do so you must add five, for Bhedia is at least five men at the same time, and at five different places. And Bhedia is like their prophet. If Bhedia says: Go left, it means bad luck for your enterprise. If Bhedia spits on a side, it's bad luck too. But if Bhedia is talking of his horses for some reason it's always good luck. Sometime Putli would like to join the gang. But Putli is never out of his father's sight. Putli knows all his father's secrets. Putli can have no friends. A snake charmer has only three friends. His oboe, his snake, and his wand. Otherwise all the universe is ash. And Putli has come to accept it: "And the Prince has come back to you, Father," says Putli walking with folded hands, straight through the astonished audiences, to his father. And never will speak a word more to anyone.

Today Mohone has gone on some errand for his family. So pockmarked Kishen is the overlord. Kishen's father is a clerk in the railways. And Kishen is always being beaten at home. His mother died some three years ago, and he and his two sisters seem to live, so to say, for the fathering of their father. Kishen has already accepted the idea of running off to Bombay with Mohone. Make money, and returning, keep the family in trim shine. They say in Bombay there are so many cinema studios, and, curl on his brow, an open shirt at the neck, flower behind his ear, Kishen is good-looking, and you could always have a part, in the films, if you are good-looking. Kishen loves Dev Anand, and he will go and say: "Star, I want to be a great actor like you. Take me." And Dev is just waiting for Kishen. On the other hand, Mohone's hero is Prithvi Raj. A hero is one who fights a battle. And Mohone loves battles. He likes even unruly cows when they kick as he milks. His father has nine cows, and the cows' milk deliberately increased with good Ganges water sold at one rupee four annas a seer. For pilgrims Ganga is holy, and so is Benares milk. One day Kishen and Mohone will take the Bombay Express at Mughal Sarai, and the people at home can beat their mounts as at their own funeral. Benares is no good for ambitious people. "What do you say to that, Bhedia?" "O, O," says Bhedia, "the red horses of Indra have no noose, for the air in Heaven is so pure one needs no noose there. And the lotuses that bloom in Heaven, the blue lotuses, are what the horses eat, and the horsegrass is eaten by man," and seeing fallen grass (from some funeral on mango packaging), Bhedia puts it into his mouth and remarks: "Sweet as sugar! Sweet as sugar!"

Mohone however had a dream. Why not take Putli with him? With Putli the trio would work better. "Hé, Dasaratha's son," you shout in the middle of the Bombay streets, and from the top of high Bombay buildings, there he comes, does Putli. "Why not steal him?" thought Mohone. Kishen liked the idea. The only thing is to follow the trace of the magician, and for this, Bhedia is the best guide. Somehow Bhedia seems to be exactly where Shalwar Khan will come. How is this you may ask?

The answer is: ask the moon? Or ask Jhaveri Bai, the fine Brahmini cow lying on the street cobblestones, chasing away her flies, shaking her ears and nibbling away at a fallen string. Some South Indian Chettiar and bought her, left her for carrying his ancestor's journey safely to the other world; and Jhaveri Bai has lived on for eight or nine years here in real regal splendour. Everybody loves her off Dashashwamedha Ghat because she is what she is. Jhaveri Bai is so gentle and civilized. Unlike the other cows she does not go and steal. She stands in front of a shop as if to say: Will you honour me? And the cow always got her mouthful of fruit or grains, unless it were some crook, and then she goes politely and stands elsewhere, thinking, thinking.

But there comes Bhedia. She also loves licking Bhedia, when Bhedia stands before her. Sometimes for hours Bhedia and Jhaveri Bai have long conversations. Bhedia stands there, his beard like a rope, and his face full of fresh scars — for once in a while Mohone and Kishen would give him a fine thrashing. And this is when his prophesies do not always come true. Bhedia after all speaks for Heaven. And the earth does not always live up to his celestial visions. So much the worse for the world. And

Bhedia never minds being beaten by children. It makes him feel fit. It makes him even happy. And when it is too painful he simply howls and all the elders come running, from the nearby building. They throw a coin at him, laugh and go away. What can you do with an idiot? Where is Mohone now? Gone? Gone? Gone.

One day Mohone and Kishen indeed disappeared. They never could take Putli with them. Perhaps someday we'll hear of them as great stars. Who knows? But for Bhedia he lost two good friends. "Now, I only have you," says Bhedia to Jhaveri Bai. "You are the Mother, and you are the Father, you are the Prince and you the charioteer. Lick me Goddess for your saliva is as honey. In Benares all dust is musk, in Benares all tears are nectar, in Benares there are no slaves and no animals! For all creatures are free. The mighty Shiva in his greatness takes his leap, and he dances. Hé, Jhaveri Bai, if you were not like Mother to me I would say, 'Marry me, for I have a horse.' A horse is no good for just a wife. But a horse is not bad you know. And he can flit from earth to Heaven within the wink of an eye. O Jhaveri Bai can you sing? I can. Listen.

> When Kanhia went to steal
> And the mountains moved
> Yasodha came from the kitchen and cried:
> 'Hé, you mischief, you diamond.'
> And hung him to her breast

Isn't that a good song? Now, come, Jhaveri Bai, sing. The boys have gone. They will throw no stones at widows or tear my beard or bring me stolen sweets, will they? I have sent them to hell. They deserve to be great stars as I deserve to be a father. Am I a father? Am I not good enough, Jhaveri Bai?"

Jhaveri Bai licks Bhedia with a love that would move men. She has such tears, she could bring the four black horses of his master, and give Bhedia back his master. What's an angry shout? All rich people shout. They think shouting is good for their throats. Lord, the humble alone are made for God. The humble who ask not like Bhedia, who beg not. "We can bathe in the Ganga and be pure." At this Jhaveri Bai gently gets up on her hind legs, whisks away a few flies, and slowly ambles down the lane to the ghats. The flies have remained behind with Bhedia. His wounds were fresh, and he did not care. Was Mohone in Bombay now, you think?

When Jhaveri Bai descends the ghats one step by one step, you feel as though the mountain was coming to the river. Jhaveri Bai sniffs the air a little, and just like a human being, she slips between pilgrims — between shaven-widows, and young married women, their shyness covered with the Ganges and wet cloth — she eats, does Jhaveri Bai, a banana peel here and there, smells a torn and forgotten towel, but before anyone has said a thing, anything, she has moved on to try and swallow some fallen pilgrim flowers. Then Jhaveri Bai looks up at the heavens, and contemplating the vast ocean which is Mother Ganga, she the daughter of the Mountains, who carries so much burden of this heavy, heavy earth — Jhaveri Bai steps one leg into the water. The flowers still hang out of her mouth. O it is so cold. Then a second step down and a third and a fourth, and sprinkling her back and face with her tail, she goes deep in till only the neck remains. Jhaveri Bai contemplates now as if she were the flow of the Ganga (and her thoughts were not far from Bhedia or the Chettiar who had offered her to God) and after she has looked across the ghats, over the pyres and the palaces and Dufferin Bridge, she shivers as if she gave up her thoughts to mother Ganga, and looks across the river to Ramnagar. Sri Rama once set his foot there on his way to fetch the great Mother Sita. Yes, the image of Him is Sweet. "Rama, Lord of the Cows," she says, "Sita Devi, mother of us, I worship you, that my sins, my friends' sins, and all evils be taken away. Birth is so mean, Death is so low. Mother give us no birth or death."

The cow's tears are purer than your brahmin prayers. Come and see it there, if you will, by the Benares ghat. "God you made the elephant and the peacock, the bear and the porcupine — even the dog did you make and the hyena, creatures of the earth. But the cow, Lord, you made as your first child. Lord, I sink in your waters, I sink into my origins, Lord give me the gift of truth."

The Ganges flows fierce and fresh on Jhaveri Bai's back. Head inturned and her horns unshaking, Jhaveri Bai contemplates her own face in the moving waters. There's magic in this picture that appears and disappears.

VI

Shankar could never speak. He could only shout. And you would hear him halfway up across the River at Ramnagar fort. In any case he could not talk to you even if he wished to. He always had to speak to the uplifted sky. A husky high voice, a rough pock-marked face, thick glasses and many swear words that he had gathered from Hindi, Kannada, Tamil (his mother tongue), Marathi (his neigbour's tongue) and even Gujarati because his father often had gujarati clients who came to consult a horoscope, and, perchance invite him to a funeral feast when the Gujarati brahmins were otherwise too busy, for Benares is a busy mart and many persons' funeral anniversaries may fall under the very same star. And this again is a mystery which someday somebody may have to clarify to Benares brahmins: why on the same day so many more die than on another day according to the celestial calendar; say around April full-moon more than around the festivities of Dussehra. There are such laws, and the brahmin has to accept this as one accepts the monsoon floods or the vivid summer heats. So many more in Gujarat and Maharashtra, in Mysore and in Peshawar have died — on exactly the same day, and on other days, the deaths are like cloud-wisps on pre-autumnal sky, you can count them, one, two, three, four, five, short, larger or elongated. To

Shankar who studied mathematics at the university, and who knew some astrology, this was all a case of "cosmological equations" as he learnedly called them. There is cosmology (which is based on geophysics) and astrology (which is based on pure numbers) and together you could make a happy mathematic and proclaim why the heaven desire (or order) the major number of deaths on one day, and such wretched few on others, so very discourteous to the brahmins of Benares.

Our friend Madhobha (of the firewood shop) is one of Shankar's friends. That is to say Shankar shouts, "Hé, Madho, what are you faking? Why don't you come down and have a smoke?" and Madhobha if he's free at all will come out and stand by the gate, and talk of anything, especially of astrology. For Madhobha, however, his interest in astrology only started when he thought his Mohini, was perhaps a wife of another life. Do such creatures exist? — one means by that, enticing subtle forms of women. He never confessed he saw a Mohini. No, Madhobha explained, he just asked because he'd heard, in his village, people speak of it. "What do I know, brother?" Shankar would shout to the street, so that the boatmen landing passengers even could hear, despite the constant lapping of the Ganges waters. "The stars are there, high up there, my dear fellow, and man is here. Two there and two here make the same. Thus there's intelligence between man and the star — through their common lingo: numbers. Hé, tell me, did you win in that bout with Abdullah? Somebody said Abdullah killed a tiger with a club when he was young. And you, you cannot even twist a cat's ear with your big, big heart." "Oh, no," says Madhobha, "When I fight, I fight. You should one day come and see me in the ring?" "Yes, I will," says Shankar.

But today Madhobha knows there's business in the air. "Brother, how are you?" asks Madhobha. "Well, well, the donkey kicks and the scorpion bites, and I smoke and shout," answers Shankar, laughing at himself. "I suppose you cannot leave the shop now." — "No, brother, there have been only three clients since the morning. That's why I could not leave when your brother Ramu came to fetch me. And the boss's daughter has the fevers. Oh, this Benares damp!" "Yes, I had some business with you," says Shankar. He now lowers his voice. His voice becomes hoarser when lowered, and seems to come in rough irregular pitches. "You see, brother, I have to pay up my exam fees. At the University, they're not our grandfathers. My only pupil has absconded to his village, and now there's not even the mite of a mice to be given lessons in mathematics!" "And how much would that be?" asks Madhobha, scratching his head, and placing his right leg on a roadside boulder. He always had pains after a bout. "I need fifty-five rupees. It's a degree exam you know. And once I pass my B.A., I can become a millionaire, if I cared to. You know I am not a fool. I have stood first in physics — well, you don't know what physics is. It is to do with the earth and the stars and so on. There was a great man, a very white man, called Newton, and he wrote some learned laws — just like, so to say, our Manu's laws. That Jaunpur Astronomical Magic House, there downtown, is no good. It smells of curdled pandits. To have precision you must have a laboratory. You must come with me one day to the University." "Yes," said Madhobha. He always thought some alchemy could help materialise his Mohini. After all look at the telephone and the aeroplane! "I said fifty-five," shouted Shankar, "but actually I need a hundred. I can't go to the examination hall in these torn clothes. Can I? They'll fail me just looking at me." True, Shankar's dhoti was torn all over and his shirt had a patch in the back.

Shankar loved to look like a Bhayya. He hated his father's paunch, his palace shawls, his clever astrology, his greed for money, and his multicoloured lies. His father told lies ten annas to the rupee. But everybody admired him. "Hé Shastri, learned Shastri," and so on. And the Hé

Shastri, learned Shastri, beat his children warm-heartedly, and sometime even threw firewood at his goddess-looking wife. He went further once and threatened to beat up his daughter-in-law, Padma, that is Shankar's wife. Padma came from Bangalore and she was the favourite among eight children. Her father was a postmaster, and he was comfortable in his own way. Three thousand rupees dowry she brought the Shastri, and Shankar was tied to her like a bull to an oil-mill. "Hoy Hoy," you want to say when you think of marriage. Woman and all that, Shankar knew even when he was a boy. What mystery could there be? Already his brother who's seventeen (and plays such excellent cricket) knows more about women than ever his grandfather did. This is of course not true for Shankar's grandfather, the great Tyagaraja Shastri who was famous for his dharma sastra learning, was also courted by important Maharajas and singers. Well, he went so often to Laxmi Bai, the singer, that rumour is that the noted Ram Lal, her son, is , as it were, a cousin of Shankar's father. The world you know is always round whatever you do with it, and the grandfather amassed a fortune reading sacred texts to Maharajas, and giving astrological consultation to concubines, and so the big Chatpadi House solidly stuck on the banks of the Ganges even rises three stories high, and you've accommodation for ten brahmin families, and at three rupees a month (pre-war rate), now thirty rupees a month (a rupee per day, new rate) they can run a kingdom on it.

The old Shastri is learned all right but nothing like his own father, neither in learning nor in goodness. Shankar is so much like him, even so. "Like grandson, like grandfather," his father used to say when on some evenings Shankar would come in, his only silk shirt shining on him, and much pan on his lips, bringing in such a powerful smell of rose-attar. "The marriage was so splendid," he shouts to his mother, who is such a goodly soul. "You had pheni and halva and silver-covered pedas. I met the bridegroom. He was a handsome, wonderful fellow." All this, every one knew, was made up. He never went to a marriage. He never met any bridegroom. But all Benares is one gup[1] — so one less or one more, who's there to care.

The father of course knew his father, so he knew his son. Where does the son get money from, became a problem. It transpired that the son was clever in wrestling bets. He applied his mathematics to astrology, and you often get the answer right, especially if you knew the horoscope of the wrestlers. And thus he made twenty or thirty rupees when he was lucky. Sometimes he was all wrong at these bets — and he would disappear, and go and watch ram-fights or cock-fights. And here, you could never know the star of the ram or the cock, brother, how could you? But you did something better. You went and watched that bearded muslim youth's face and you could say he was capricorn (sometimes western astrology also helped). Or that other middle-aged cockster was a leo. When leo meets capricorn who wins unless that day the other stars were all wrong for the leo, etc., etc.

And then also, Shankar shouted his lessons in mathematics to his pupil. This brought him twenty or twenty-five rupees a month, and it made up his college fees and his bus or bicycle hire, and a coffee or milk came in by the way.

However, since Padma came into the house, everything was changed. Padma was Padma herself, a lotus-born, and such a gentle, civilized, sweet-voiced girl for this "barbarian Benares brahmin," he would say of himself. Since the day she came the aspect of the house changed, or so it would seem. His mother loved her first daughter-in-law, and Padma this, and Padma that, made the whole house sing. Sometimes sitting in his class of physics or mathematics, Shankar would suddenly think of Padma, and forget his electrodes before him or the notebook. For

---

1. gossip.

Shankar, who knew only how to shout, sometimes fell into compounded silences. At those moments he lost all consciousness of classroom, Benares or Shankar, and be in the real nowhere. Perhaps far away on some other star, or constellation, in some other universe, or just because of a mathematical formula — he felt silence within himself. And nothing moved. He loved these moments. He had them more and more often after Padma came. And when Padma fell at the feet of "this barbarian Benares brahmin" or the 3Bs as he called himself, he instinctively felt like falling at his wife's feet in return. How can virtue fall at the feet of vice? So he'd rise and stand, and sometimes suddenly he entered into that august silence. There he saw no one, no, none. Nowadays, he did not even sit for his prayers. This silence could not come from any god, though he believed in God. "Aré," he would shout, "God is there, and whatever we do, he's like that Moti Ram of the bicycle shop. He hires you his bicycle, even if you haven't paid him for three months. 'Take it and pay it when you like,' he says. God hires us his bicycles and we pay for it when we go to heaven. Here you enjoy, and there you pay," he would shout and become silent again.

But since Padma came God is no more a bicycle hirer. God has gone up because without telling any one Shankar would come back with flowers behind his ears, and a sanctified coconut in his hands. Yes, he'd been to Vishwanathji's temple. "Mother here is prasad. Hé Padma, I have been to Vishwanathji. What do you say to that? May you prosper." *"Their[2]* prosperity," she says in her deep-set gentle voice, "is my riches." "Yes, yes. But I'm no millionaire. You were brought up on silks. Mother!" and he suddenly shouts, "I am hungry." Thus day by day after Padma entered this household he became less and less of a 3B, and everybody wondered. You never smelt perfume

---

2. An orthodox Hindu woman never mentions her husband's name and always refers to him in third person plural.

anymore on him or the sporting of a silk shirt, unless he took mother and Padma to a cinema. He smoked heavily. This he could not stop. How could he? How could he be less of a barbarian: Could the pock-marks change on his face? Could he be anything but a brahmini bull of the Ganga ghat?

Sitting by the Ganges on an autumnal evening, sometimes with his wife and his mother, but often alone, and looking at the auspicious curve Mother Ganga takes down by Rajghat and temple lights which bring bounty to dusk, and while the drums are silenced by the sudden night, Shankar would think: Yes, he would become a business man. Perhaps a business magnate. One day he would go overseas. (His father may vituperate against his first-born. Pray, how could a brahmin go across the dark waters? But even bad fathers like good luck for their sons. After all you could always drink some Ganges water, after your return, say a few mantras, and become brahmin again.) He saw, did Shankar, a series of mills, cotton mills, ginning and weaving exquisite muslin cloth — you know, like snow, almost like those our weavers wove before the British came. Shankar would run the mill on modern economic methods. That is why he decided he'd a study economics for his M.A. With mathematics, economics is an easy play. Economics is just simian sense plus hard numbers. Shankar had some rational sense, and knew a lot about numbers. Also he drew his own chart. Mercury was in the sixth house (and Venus in the seventh) while sun was in the tenth. The trigone makes for business, and even for big business. His knowledge of Gujarati, Tamil, and Hindi would help besides his smattering of Bengali might be of use in Calcutta. The British would one day go — they are preparing to quit anyway (though Shankar played safe, and wore no khadi, and was no Congress volunteer) — and all big business will fall into Indian hands. Prepare from now, and you will win.

Padma brought luck. There's no doubt about it. She with her Monday fasts and her Friday evening worships, she brought light to this darksome house. And Shankar could not but be a big man, and one evening a clucking wall-lizard even confirmed these hopes.

"Let's go home," he shouted to his mother and wife. He'd forgotten his cinema. But the wife and mother were not there. After worshipping at the little shrine of Tribhuvana (just on the Harischandra Ghat, some yards down the steps, from their house) they had gone home to prepare the dinner. And a mere few nights later, as if to prove Padma would bring in prosperity, she whispered to him: "I think it's there." "What's there!" shouted Shankar sitting up, laying aside his glasses and text books. "Hé, what's there, Padma? Speak!" — "Oh may *they* be unperturbed. I thought this evening, that may be something's happening to me." — "Happening to you, Padma, what? Are you ill? Have you the fevers, the coughs, or the furoncles, or what?" "Oh, nothing, nothing at all," whispered Padma trying to pull her husband back to silence. "Oh just this," she said after a moment's hesitancy. (Whenever Shankar wanted to think, even in darkness, he needed his thick glasses. So he lay his glasses on his nose again, thinking and thinking.) Finally his mind left her, and what she had said, and suddenly jumped on to some problem of University physics. That Schrodinger equation was all a mess of molasses, and he could not understand what was what. However, he would have to go to sleep now and wake early and study. Books are learnt better during early morning hours than in the mid-night. Anyway when one has a dance head like Shankar has, Shankar said to himself, one has no hope except drive cattle to village pastures! Hé!

But suddenly remembering his wife had said something to him, he sat up and asked: "Padma, what's the illness? Tell me. You know I can take you to Dr. Pandurang (whose father knew my grandfather) or to the civil surgeon Dr. Stake, MRCP, FRCS, an eminent doctor, or even to Hakim Abdullah. We are well placed here for every form of medical treatment, Allopathic, Ayurvedic, Unani.

And because of our family there will be no difficulty in getting any one. Any bloke you want who carries those stethoscopes and pinch-me pinch-me-not witcheries of the syringe, a Pandit who gives you trichurations of pearl or a Hakim that makes you swallow dung-smelling confections. Anything you like!" "No doctor is needed," remarked Padma, laughing. "Every woman's her own doctor." "You mean you have menstrual troubles," he shouted like he would say: "I want my match box. Hé fetch it for me." "Oh no," she whispered. "I think we're going to have a son." And Shankar jumped up, put on the light (they had electricity in the house) and for some reason slipped on his silk shirt, and wept. He never thought such good fortune would come to him. "What, to this 3B, a son?" A son. A real puling little son. Beat the drum and proclaim. "Hé, ring the temple bells and proclaim Shankar Narayan Shastri Dravida is going to have a son. His wife has just conceived. Hé jump up. Leap up." And he said to his wife: "May I bring you a glass of milk?" "No," said Padma, "It's late in the night, let us go to sleep." "Asleep after what you have revealed to me. A butcher may go to sleep after a slaughter, a tax-collector after fleecing his client. But a brahmin boy dances with joy when a son is conceived by his spouse. Are you all right?" he asked, trying to pat her on the stomach. "All right, all right, I mean," he repeated — "Why yes, no, it's not a sickness. Why should I be sick?" "I meant," shouted whisperingly Shankar, "You may need something? Some halva, peda or something sweet to eat, milk to drink. You may have cravings and demands." "Oh, no yet," said Padma trying to get her husband back to bed. "Not yet. It's perhaps only the second month." "Quick work you've done my wife," he shouted. The mother knocked at the door. "Is there anything wrong, Padma?" — "No, mother. You know how *They* are. *They* are just restless. May *They* go to sleep. All is all right."

But try as he might Shankar could not go to sleep. How go to sleep when this cosmological event is taking place, as it were, before your very eyes: like the creation of a planet or a galaxy, like some star-spark broken from a planet and falling into empty space, one minute sperm has got stuck with one oviodal cell in the nowhere of space, and there's going to be splendid son, a great son. "We'll call him Vishwanath," he said to himself. "Vishwanath Shastri, hé Vishwanath Shastri?" he queried, caressing her stomach, "will you be a pandit or a scientist or a business man?" "A pandit like his grandfather, a scientist like his father, and a business man because of himself," she said. — "No, no, Padma, I am restless. I must do something immediately!" And before she knew where he was he jumped out on the veranda. After all she could not run after him. It's just not done. Where was he going? What is he doing?

He came back late, late in the silences of the night. He'd gone to the temple straight and had taken peda and jasmines with him. There was a large crowd because it was processional day, of some sort. He sat with the pilgrims, and sang his part of the Shiva *stotram:* "I may be no orthodox brahmin," he shouted to Padma later, "but I know how to articulate my *anya* and my *jnya*," and he started his *stotram* again.

Kashika puradhi natha
Kalabhairavam bhajeth. Kalabhairavam bhajeth.

The Lord of the city of Kashi
Kalabhairavam I praise.

"And I went to the Ganga and said: Mother Ganga you will have to give me a son. He must be better than me. He must be much much better than me. He must neither smoke nor drink nor womanise. He must be pure (*aparna*) and great. And I threw some flowers at Mother Ganga. And you know how the Mother does, when she answers. She hissed her two-lipped hiss, as if she said the same thing twice over. When Mother Ganga is there what lack of greatness," he remarked and wept between his knees. Then he added as if to himself: "I am a sinner, and I am going to have a son. I hope he has neither gonorrhea nor syphilis. I am cured of both." "Oh slowly, slowly?" pleaded Padma. "The elders are asleep." "I speak to the walls, to these ancestral walls," he cried. "They know me and I know them. Walls, walls, makes my son good. Make him eminent. Don't make him a Gandhi-gander. He must be virile and bright. Make him worthy of Padma," he said, and as if in a sudden frenzy took hold of his wife's two feet, and sobbed and sobbed. "A sinner, Padma, touched his wife's holy feet." — "Oh, may *They* not do such inauspicious things. Please, please, I'm just a country chit." The Vishwanath temple gongs struck and cleared the air, as if for all time. A large lit emptiness fell over holy Benares. Then something suddenly happened to Shankar. He hurled himself on the bed and fell fast asleep next to his wife. The Temple prasad lay at their head. He felt for the first time intrepid.

It was the next day he sent his younger brother Ramu who lived at the university campus to Madhobha. Madhobha always lent him money whenever Shankar needed any. "It's God's money and anybody can return it as long as he returns it to God," remarked Madhobha. As everybody knew Madhobha would one day retire to his village and build a temple to Shiva, and with marble steps going down to the deep transparent temple tank, and four big marble lions at the four entrances to the waters. There would be a large Sadhu's quarters, a pilgrim house, and may be even food for the travellers. It all depends on how much silver there would be in the box, and he just does not know. And then lying on the steps of the temple he would hear his Mohini sing. It should be the full moon and the waves of the tank would gently caress the marble steps. Hé Shambo.

"My wife," shouted Shankar, as if it was a truth so big all Benares should know: "My wife is going to have a son, and I need money for the third month ceremony, the seventh month ceremony, and the delivery, and where will I find it till the university students return after the holidays and I have a worthy pupil? Next year I'll take two," he said, "for my wife must have all her pregnancy-desires fulfilled." Whenever it concerned women, Madhobha had a generous heart. "Come tonight, not now," said Madhobha, "and if I'm not here, wait for me. I will have the hundred rupees ready. You give it back to me before the child is born. Understood. That is by November or December. Latest. Before the Shiva festival. Understood. That gives you enough time."

Shankar shouted: "You are a saintly fellow, meant to be looking at your nose and navel and not be selling firewood for the dead. The world, brother, is all upside down."

"Somebody has to sell firewood for the dead," said Madhobha. "I or another Madhobha, it's just the same. As long as you have Shiva in your heart, all's well."

"When is your next bout?"

"Next Wednesday."

"Grand show?" asked Shankar.

"Perhaps. I face Manilal of Rampur."

"That rascal. He deserves to be in prison. The way he does all the wrong slips and hits. He's no boxer, he's a butcher."

"The good have to be going on being good. The rest God takes care of," said Madhobna and that's when the boss called, so Madhobha said: "We'll meet tonight," and disappeared. Then Shankar went to all the shops of the city. He wanted to buy a ruby nose-ring for his wife. She had one in diamond, people had given her at the wedding. But for the gift of the child, a husband should give at least a ruby nose-ring. He wandered all afternoon as if he were the richest man in Benares. He was going to be a business man, of this there could be no doubt now, and the sound of factories would send him to sleep. Hé, what do you say to that, brother? Speak! He now consulted jeweller after jeweller, and one shop had it. Just *it*, the right ruby for Padma. You know a ruby must say, "I belong to Padma," just as a horse says, "I belong to Moti Ram." Despite physics and all that Shankar believed in the personality of precious stones. The true ones brought good luck, and the evil ones calamities. So this ruby nose-ring, and for thirty-five rupees, he would take it this evening, place it before Annapurna Devi at the temple, have a thousand-and-eight-namings-of-the-name done. And with the prasadam and the jewel you go home as if you have drunk the milk of the white cows of Vrindavan.

"Mother," he said, coming in after he had washed his feet and placed the prasadam and the jewel (in its neat little carboard box) before the family deity. The lamps burned cherub bright, and all seemed such true peace. "Mother, your daughter-in-law is going to have a baby." And Padma hearing this came and fell at the Mother-in-law's feet.

"May you bear a hundred sons," she blessed and she blessed again touching the back of the daughter-in-law's head. Then Padma went in and fell before the family deity.

"Open the box," shouted Shankar.

"Why? There's no hurry," whispered Padma.

"There is hurry. I am a 3B but I know how to recognise the worth of my first born. Open and see, Padu."

"Open, daughter," cried the Mother-in-law. The daughters of the house — Shankar had two sisters, one five and another nine years of ago — they were chanting their studies. They were studying geography in Hindi, and an English poem.

"Open and see," repeated the Mother-in-law.

Padma opened the box, fell before the gods and coming to her husband in pride, fell at his feet again.

"May our son be pure," he said as if it was the language

of his ancestors. Yes, what more could man need? And going before his family deity he fell prostrate and sobbed, "Mother Annapurna, take away my sins, my million, million sins. O mother!" Then he rose and fell prostrate before his own mother. "Where is father?" he shouted, rising. "Coming back from Rai Singha Singh Bahadur!" No sooner the father came he fell, did Shankar, at his father's feet and said: "My wife is pregnant."

"May she bear a hundred sons," blessed the father. Padma now came and fell at his feet. He repeated: "Daughter, may you live a hundred years and bring prosperity to your husband."

The truth of life is just this. After the meal Shankar went back to his room and started reading his big book on chemistry. Strong in physics, he was weak in chemistry. He blamed his professor, but the fact was he liked numbers better. You could work magic with numbers, but chemistry was so much fireworks. All this messy test tube business was too dirty and dangerous. Poisonous fumes and coloured gases, they looked like breathings of the very devil. After the show is over you have only the empty shells left. In mathematics you climb mountains. Mathematics is therefore like the Himalayas. The higher you go the holier it becomes. And near Kailas, on the snowy heights, and from Gangotri does the Mother Ganga emerge. "Zero is Ganga, Ganga is zero," he shouted as if he'd discovered a Vedic mantra. I tell you, you could grind castor pods at the hell-mill, the Ganga beside you. The Ganga purifies all. She gives song to the songstress, limbs to the brave, paddle-push to the boat, and child to the wife. "O giver of gifts Ganga Mata," says Shankar to himself, and in prayer, closes firm his eyes.

Padu came in late tonight, the Mother-in-law had rheumatism and so Padu cleaned up the kitchen all alone. Padu brings the glass of milk for the night. A pregnant wife and silver tumbler of milk, Lord, what more does a man want? "And the ruby is so right," he says as he looks gratefully at her. And the milk smelt of almonds and of saffron and of fine good camphor. "A civilized wife civilizes a barbarian," he said and laughed. The walls seemed warmed and quiet. His son would have no name. No, he will have a name: "$E=MC^2$."[3]

"How do you like that, Padu?" he shouted, and hearing no answer listened to the flow of the River, and deeply fell into sleep.

---

3. $E=MC^2$: In relativity theory, it represents "Energy is equal to M-mass x c^2—the square of the speed of light."

VII

*B*holanath was from Rajgarh, district Ghazipur. He was one of eleven children — ten boys and one precious girl. She was born some years before Bhola, and, Shiva-Shivah, was Sati not arrayed in red, mirror-worked cholis and skirts, with a nose-ring of ruby, and earrings of corrugated silver? They bought her a sari when she was but seven years old — such her natural felicity.

Father Goraknath was a wheelwright by profession, and on the Benares-Ayodhya road, in those days, were there not, tell me, many, many bullock carts? And he also helped in the shoeing of bulls. The stars were good, the roads were active and all went well, and soon good Sati was married off to the son of a neighbouring peasant, Rajnath. But Sati was not meant for living. She died giving birth to a puling little boy that latter grew up to be a stalwart of the village; he could fight every pugilist in town and down the adversary in the beat of an eye. They called him Bhim because he was so valourous, and soon everyone forgot his real name — for he was in truth called, on birth, Banarasidas[1]. And Bhim was in every party that went on marketing expeditions up to the elephant-fair at Sonapur, in

---

1. Banarasidas—Devotee of Benares, a fairly common name all over north India.

Bihar — one took twelve days of the bullock cart to reach there, but it was so gay, and Rai Krishnadas of Rampur village, the elderly Zamindar next door, sometimes bought an elephant, and Bhim was the Zamindar's faithful hero and guard. Thus Bhim drove the bullock-cart, and Rai Krishnadas went in this huge, noisy, creaking vehicle, with two white bulls, and a merry procession it was that went, past Ghazipur and Ballia and then on to Sonapur. You drank a lot, and you meddled with a woman or two, here and there, and you brought back an elephant and a horse or even two elephants and many horses, according to your purse or your phantasy — and this was always much fun. Bholanath too (some three or four years younger than Bhim — for Bhola, the uncle, was born after many miscarriages of his ailing mother, and that's why they called him Bhola, the brave) — accompanied his nephew but one day while the two stalwarts who looked so like the Pandava brothers, Nakula and Sahadeva, well then, when they were returning from the Sonapur fair (but, this time, Rai Krishnadas bought no elephant), some uniformed men overtook them a few miles out of Gauripur, drafted them, giving them big shoes, uniform and gun, and sent them soon, very soon, across the darkling waters. And how Rati sobbed when she heard this, for they had been married but for three thin months. Bhim, however, died somewhere on the sand dunes near Bizerte, and Bholanath became expert in fixing carwheels (and remember, he was a wheelwright's son, and some good company commander discovered this castecraft of Bholanath) and when the company was sent to Italy first and then on to Flanders (a small company of machine men), he went with them, and being far in the farthest camp, and not in the trenches, he escaped death. After all death had taken his dues with the three stillborn before him, and with Bhim, his twin as it were dead, Bholanath would live a hundred years. And there would always be Rati for him.

Bhola had one passion, however. He used to love songs — not filmy songs, no, but kirtans, songs of God. He remembered his Tulsi Das in Flanders, and Pandit Viswanath who was the company cook, big tummy, sacred-thread, great temper and all; though a brahmin, he cooked *everything* yet was he not a safe vegetarian? He also possessed an ancient and much worn copy of Tulsi Ramayan. So day after day after starting campfire on those cold autumnal nights, Bholanath and Vishwanath read out the holy story to the assembled soldiers, and people wept on the Flanders plains, thinking on the suffering of Sita in exile, and under Ravana's power. You remember the text, don't you? where Hanuman, the monkey-god, from up the Asoka tree, sees Mother Sita, and she so seated in grief and thinking on the lotus feet, the Padmapada, of her husband, Sri Rama, while Ravana arrives there promising that Mandodari and all his queens, would be her handmaids, if only Sita would look on him but once, and how, posing a blade of grass, as partition, between this ten-headed monster and her withdrawn self, she mocks at that absurd and vain scoundrel, replying in answer, could a lotus ever blossom because of a firefly's glow? And here all the soldiers laughed and laughed. But Ravana rushes towards her, in a paroxysm, his sword lifted bright, shouting, "I will cut off your head, you understand." But Sita Devi, when she addresses the sword prayerfully, saying, "you sharp and cool and kind blade, please dispel my grave weight of dukha, sorrow caused by this desperate separation from my Lord, the Lord of the Raghus," and hearing which how all the soldiers began to sniffle and sob into their blankets, while the fire shot up in pure celestial worship. "He who touches Devi Sita's footsteps even in thought is freed from a thousand births," wrote Tulsi Das, and Ravana, the wretch, knew it. Yet such is human existence: you vomit on what you worship. Who can protect you ever from your primal destiny, unless it be Sri Rama himself. Ravana had to be killed to attain liberation, so Ravana had to abduct Sita. Thus alone could Ravana's head be on Sri Rama's feet. And this was all the play of Sri Rama himself, he, Sri Rama, the very fount of compassion, explains Pandit Vishwanathji, that gave greenness to the trees, and the long waist for the mother-monkey to carry her young, he also gave Ravana such love that Ravana feared and hated his Lord. Has not Tulsi Das said, when Mandodari asks him, he, Ravana who could take any shape he wished, such his magic powers, why, she asked, did he not impersonate Sri Rama himself to seduce Sita, and tell me, did not Ravana the monster reply, "The moment I think of Him, Sri Rama, I become his devotee and lie at his perfumed feet." For hate is only love standing upside down — get it back on its feet, like a single-footed lead doll that you can buy at any village fair, which returns on itself, explains Pandit Vishwanathji, do what you will do with it, such too is love, it returns always on itself. And the soldiers always wept for Mother Sita, and prayed that evil Ravana be forgiven. Thus they prayed for Hitler too across the enemy lines. They had heard Hitler was a vegetarian and a celibate: tell me, what more could one need to be called a devotee of the Lord?

And when the bhajan was over Pandit Vishwanath kept Bhola near him and talked to him of Bhakti and Brahman, and though all this flew beyond his head, especially as he was often called out in the middle of the discourses to repair a tank-wheel or a truck-axle, and even sometimes the trigger of a machine-gun. Bholanath, however, pursued his readings. On the plains of Flanders he learnt the *Shiva stotra* by heart, and the Chandi hymns (the Pandit had also bought a copy of the *Brihat Stotra Ratnakara* with him) and so hammering his wheels or patching his tyre you would hear Bhola chant.

gangatarangamaniya jatakalapam
gauriniranatravibhushitavamabhagam.
narayanapriyamanagamadapaharam
varanasipurapathih bhaja vishwanathan.

Worship Vishwanath, the Lord of Benares,
Whose locks seem delightful with wavelets of

the Ganga,
He who is ever adorned on his left with
Mother Gauri,
(He again) beloved of Narayana,
And the conqueror of the Bodiless God (Kama).

And when finally they came to the epilogue of Tulsi Ramayan, how they all wept, while they remembered Shiva himself had requested Garur, the Eagle-Lord, to go to Kakabhusundi, the Jewel among the Crows, and hear the sweet story of Sri Rama, as the Crow told the story day after day to the assembled birds, and how Garur explains, already at the sight of the Nilagiris, the Blue mountains, Maya fell off from all his five perceptions, and then taking his bath at the nearby river, and going up to the great banyan tree, sees Bhusundi, surrounded by all the varied birds and Bhusundi, asks: "Oh, King of the Feathered World," in great humility and gestures of etiquette, "with what intent, and how is it you have betaken yourself our way," to which, Garur makes the reply: "Lord Shiva himself sent me that I hear the Holy Tale of the Acts of Sri Rama from you. Yet just looking at you was enough, my doubts and misjudgements have all vanished." On hearing which such holy joy filled the heart of Bhusundi, that he related to the King of Birds, the geneaology of Sri Rama's family, from Raghu downwards, — the arrival of the sage Vishwamitra to arrange the marriage of the Lord to Sita Devi, daughter of one King of Videha, the abduction of Mother Sita by Ravana the monster, and of the monkeys that helped Sri Rama to build the bridge across the ocean and conquer the vast island of Lanka, then the killing of Ravana and of the flight back of Rama and Sita to Ayodhya in an aerial chariot of flowers, ending with the blissful coronation of Sri Rama. "O King of Birds," concluded Bhusundi, "Even Maya, you know, dances on the brow of Sri Rama. Such is Sri Rama, who is Knowledge, Bliss and Truth." And then, with the image of Sri Rama in his heart, and bowing low to Bhusundi, how Garur flew up to the Vaikuntha Heaven, to lie forever and ever at Sri Vishnu's Feet, Sri Rama being none else than Sri Vishnu who took the human form for our redemption from Maya.

Then Pandit Vishwanath always ended his readings with: "He who hears this story and tells this story of Sri Rama to another, were it a man, bird or animal, will be blessed by Sri Rama. So, now let us chant,

Raghupathi Raghava Raja Ram,
Pathitha Pavana Sita Ram,"

The Lord of the Raghus, Raghava, King Rama,
Redeemer of the fallen, Sita's Rama.

and this chant filled the cold wet air of Flanders, day after day, with an utter sweetness. And they returned to their tents in deep peace, even as the war went on, above and before them, and they sometimes wondered, which war was which, here or there. For everything on earth, the good and the bad, come to the one single end — touching the holy feet of Sri Rama.

The war will soon be over and Bhola would return home and be with Rati, again. What was he going to do returning to Rajgarh village, he wondered. The old father was dead (he had died of the new war fevers that killed so many many), and a few days later, so the letters from Rati said, the third son Digambar had died, and one or two days later, Pitambar of the same epidemic. The mother was left with only eight sons and their children — some drove bullock-carts to carry merchandise, others worked for Rai Krishnadas with his new puff-puff textile mills, and yet others had run away to Delhi and Bombay to find war work, for, your must know, the German war brought work, and work paid. Once in a while Urmili (the mother) got her money order from one or the other of her sons, was it from Bombay or Kanpur or Calcutta, but these began to come less and less. When you go far you forget where you came from. To love you must stay where you were first suckled. What is love if you cannot know how many calves, Rani, the big white cow of your Mother's yard has had, or of the big floods of the Ganga, years ago when over a thousand people had died, or remember the small-pox years when your little niece Madhuri had been carried down to the ghats. Of course there was his Rati — she came originally from Vidwanpur in the Beli Tehsil, and she was the only daughter of a rich peasant who had a mistress and had played with her, had even took her to Sonapur fair — in fact it's there Bholanath's father and he had met and that's how Bhola and Rati were duly married — well, Rati, was not beautiful like her name but she knew how to cook and stitch, plaster cow-dung over the walls, draw water from the deep, dark well in the backyard, — but was ever, ever silent. She never said one lone word to anyone in pain or in happiness. She never complained. She never even said she would like to go home to her mother, for the autumnal festivities. After all she could have gone, for her husband was far away at the war, but she would not do this to his family. She sat in prayer often that her Lord come back, then they will duly have a child. How the womb calls for its child. All her sisters-in-law had more children than they wanted but she had not during her two years of marriage, given birth to, were it, a little baby monkey. Even a scorpion is worth bearing for a woman than one be childless, that's how the saying goes. A childless woman brings ill luck. Women will not invite you to their houses. They will not even look at you, lest your inauspicious gaze fall on them, and make them thus forever barren. Lord what has one done that this should be so? But Bhola will come back soon and she will have a male child.

Bhola comes back, and with the grace of Mother Ganga, he returned just as he had gone. The dark waters had given him no roughness nor did he drink. He talked of Rama and Sita, even more so now. And he always talked of Pandit Vishwanath. Bhola never told a lie. He joined the wheelwright work, and now that cars began to be made in this country, people heard of him here — they heard of him there — and he became a motor mechanic to the Zamindar families of Ghazipur. Sometimes at a grand marriage they would even ask him to drive a car for the nuptial procession (there were not so many car drivers either in those days) and often Bhola could even tame a rutting elephant (he had learnt this from an Elephant-merchant at Sonapur fair), with half a bucket of prithi grass-juice for the stomach and chilli putties pasted on the forehead. His fame spread, but you always heard him repeating some mantra. And three years after his arrival his wife's girth showed roundness, and in a few months a baby boy was indeed born to Bholanath. Life is so simple: God gives when He gives. For the rest man has to say his mantras assiduously, eat good food, sleep, wake and work. Since the Lord gave the child, Bholanath called the boy Vishwanath because that was the name of his teacher in Flanders, and also, of course, of Shiva in Benares. And soon Bhola put the household bulls to the yoke and with grandmother, mother, and the child, ringing the bells, the cart sped towards holy Benares.

What happened after that Bholanath will not tell you. He will turn towards his Guru and smile. And the Guru (whom you now realise to be Vishwanathji) says in grave benignance: "Well, who knows, sir, the ways of the Lord!" Bholanath had come to Benares with his family, and no sooner than they arrived at the sacred city than a virulent epidemic of cholera broke out. The mother and the wife died almost the same day. The child lived three days further, and it sank too in his arms to death. Bhola came to the river with this little body in his arm — it was night and he wanted to let the child float down, a gift to the Ganges, "let mother Ganga who gave him to us, take him too," he wanted to say. But God intervened as he always does for a devotee in distress. Vishwanathji himself appeared. "I was there," explains Vishwanathji to any pilgrim who wants to hear the story, "I was there, seated on the Dashashwamedha Ghat. I had just come from Calcutta having resigned my job. I had been a clerk at the Patent Office. My train came at eight o'clock (she was late by four hours) and after throwing in my luggage at a dharmasala, I rushed to Mother Ganga. I took my bath in the holy river, and sat on the steps of the ghats. As I sat contemplating her, I recognised Bhola at once, the dead child in Bhola's arms, and a full moon on the heavens. I stopped him from giving the child to the Ganga. I bought firewood and had the child duly burnt. That's the way to really deal with the dead and once for all, so. And," concluded Vishwanathji, "Bhola never went back to Rajgarh."

The Sadhu gives you a loving smile. "Then I took on the ochre, and Bhola continued to stay with me. He goes to work at the Imperial Motor Works — Bhola patches a tyre or twists a plug, he's magical with the machine. And the car purrs and darts off. He gets well paid for it. He brings me rice and vegetables and firewood," says the Sadhu, gently patting his thighs. "He looks after me out, and I look after him in."

Bhola, his fingers covered with foulest grease, hides his face with his large quiet hands. "I'm no one to look after any one. The great Vishwanath high up there looks after every one in the world, and this Vishwanath here looks after me."

"But, Bholanath, you mean you will end your days, like this, on the Ganga Ghat?"

"As Dadu says, 'Home is Ganga Ghat for he who's even once the Ganga hath seen. Never a home be a home where Mother Ganga floweth by not."

"But you are not very old yet. Why this thin-limbed asceticism?"

"Man lives for happiness, as Vishwanathji says. And if happiness is on the Ganga I say take it, eat it, be submerged in it, as you're with the Ganga. Sometimes when the red dawn breaks on the Ganga, I cannot bear the veiled white silence over the river — it brings tears to my eyes. I do not know why, but never for father or mother have I wept as I do for the Ganga — this Ganga is my father, this Ganga is my mother. I've seen the world and its ways, I've seen the wars of the Redman, the glory of Rome, the gaiety of Paris. For me, the service of my Guru comes first. And what could be of deeper worth than performing the services of the Guru on the Ganga Ghat. I tell you brother: Never is there greater joy for man than that his Guru and his Ganga be side by side. Hé, hara-hara Shambho."

And Bholanath lights his hooka, and looks sadly at the world. A monkey is picking the lice off her neighbour. Some middle-aged widow is slipping into the Ganga for her bath. She has strong limbs but her sparse hair is white. The children are teasing an old woman seated on the Ganga, a cloth bundle beside her: "Hé, hé, where's your husband?" — "And how many teeth have you in your mouth?" — "Thirty-two," says another. And they all burst into laughter. Bholanath rushes toward the boys, a fuel stick in hand, and frightens them away. And as a funeral is coming, Bholanath goes over and drives off the crows and the vultures from the pyre-platform. If there's one nuisance in a Benares death, it's the crows. And every crow is not a Kakabhusundi.

You can now see Bhola's Guru light his oven and put a lid on the cooking vessel, and while Bhola keeps the monkeys away, the Guru slips into the water for his midday bath. He who has not slipped into the Ganges and felt the lightness of the Ganges knows not water. You plunge and plunge again into the Ganga. And you are suddenly aware of a fragrance of holiness and the touch of a deep white truth. And when you spit that water out, how your belly gurgles in happiness.

When the Guru returns, Bhola goes down the ghat. Bhola will now sit, a pipal twig in hand, his left leg in the water, his head resting on the other knee, doodling away on the steps of the ghat. He goes drawing a triangle first, and then dipping the twig in the Ganga brings it back quickly surrounding the triangle with a circle, and rubbing it away, starts all over again.

"What's that, Bhola," I ask.

"Birth, marriage and death — my story has three parts, and here," he says drawing the circle round around the triangle, "is God."

"You were born a wheelwright...," I start saying.

"Yes, yes," he interrupts, "yes, you see, God himself is a potter. He made the wheel from which came this pot," and he laughs, beating his chest with dire conviction. "Brother, all ends in a circle," he repeats and throws a stone to drive away a crow, and hop-hop it disappears. Then dipping the twig into the Ganga he makes the triangle and the circle again. "Till the triangle become the circle, you see, God will not be pleased." And then he sits cross-legged murmuring to himself:

Agar Gangaji na kahé to
Kon japéga Ram,
Agar mein na kahé to,
Tuhi rahéga Ram (!)

If the Ganga does not say
Who then will go on naming Ram,
If I do not say (!)
You alone will remain, O Ram.

VIII

"Palki, Palki," the whisk-bearer would shout, running reverentially through the squeezing-in, stony tumbling-forth lane, "Palki, Palki, the Palki of Rani Rasomani. Hé, make way, make way, ye strangers," and the head palanquin bearer, red-turban, and silver bangle on left arm, will sing,

> The parrot has no teeth
> The hen no crown
> The fig hath no flower
> Nor the river a back-going step.

"No back-going step," shout the chorus.

> Shiva took poison and hung it in his throat,
> Parvathi sat in meditation that Shiva open his eye.
> Make way, make way, ye auspicious strangers.
> Even the barren woman could have a child if
>   Shiva willeth.

And all the Benares crowd looked back, and then looked forward as the palanquin bearers rushed down the lanes, and looking in, people could see a husk-skinned, aged woman in a white sari, white hair spread sparse over her forehead, with a fixed stare, and saying her beads. She seemed unconcerned as to what she saw or heard — for her the world was made this way since the day of Brahma's creation, and it would go on thus until the final dissolution and flood — and that takes, you know, a million million man-years. Nothing in Benares has ever changed since Shiva decided to come down and emerge here for the benefit of mankind, on this crescent curve where the two streams Varuna and Asi meet, and the stalls and the lanes, even the dustbins and the curs were for Rani Rasomani, primordial creations. She did not feel so, she knew so. Where the truth is, nothing changes.

In fact Rani Rasomani was herself born a widow. That she had a husband is true.

Hé, hé ye auspicious strangers,
Make way as the palanquin moves forth.

But that was so long ago that one forgets him, as it were, although, of course, he was ever present in the household. How could he not be? The truth about the dead is just this. They are dead and forgotten, but they seem to hide behind rice-sacks, in broomstick corners, by the shade of the tamarind tree, in the courtyard, under bedsteads, in the eyes of servants' children, in between two bamboo-tassellated fans of the attendants — the dead man sat by you at meals but did not eat — you could almost hear the gluglutonating sounds of his digestion, as he rubs his belly, and yet he was all somewhat smoke and air. That was why it seemed so long ago — thus now, now. And for Rani Rasomani, her husband, His Highness Raja Protapachandra Mozumdar, Raja of Bankipur, was like a temple tank or a mountain you've visited on pilgrimage, as a child. It is always there and yet it is not here. You understand. This made the stare so steady, and the prayer so easy.

Make way ye God-hunters
Make way and rush to your chase
The deer has much ear

> The panther much limb
> The neel-gai has no courage
> For God made it such
> You hunt only Him
> Him only you hunt.

Rani Rasomani still remembers her husband. It was just like the other day, Lord Curzon gave parties every evening — every other evening, so to say, and Raja Protapachandra rejoiced in drink. He loved the Europeans for that sake. He would go, would the Raja, with turban and achkan and all, and come back without turban and achkan, Mohan Singh, the Sikh driver, almost carrying him in his arms. The Raja was a delicate man. He had been to England when young for a holiday, and came back so full of European manners. He was presented to Edward VII. And since then he wore cuff links with the pictures of Edward VII engraved on them. The Raja of Bankipur, Rani Rasomani remembers, was also learned in music. Who in Calcutta society did not love music? The Raja was no exception. Only he loved the Parsi-theatre songs. He went to every play of the Parsi-theatre, and he shed many a tear for Bilva Mangal.[1] His father, the great Sir Apurvachandra Nityanand Mozumdar, KCSI, CIE was still alive, and once in a while the father-in-law would ask the third son, for that was what Protapachandra was, to go to Bankipur by boat — Bankipur was on the Maha Ganga — and check accounts, examine the cattle, one and all, or simply go and see if the peasants were keeping the canal cleared properly and if their kids were looked after hygienically. The old Raja was a man of ideas. He had been a Brahmo since he was born (his father knew Keshub) and so the house was filled with the songs of enlightenment. The brahmin was strictly not allowed in the drawing room. He would go through the side door, to the lady's quarters, but, here

---

1. A romantic operatic play.

among men, God has neither hands nor feet.

> Make way, make way, ye strangers
> The waterpot does not get filled without help,
> The village tank not overflow without rain,
> The baby does not come before the ninth-month
> And God cometh not till the puzzle be solved
> Left nor right, man nor woman, object nor Brahman.
> Make way make way ye strangers.

But the God of the women's quarters lives on astrological readings, on delicious food offered to Him which He does not eat but the brahmins gulp with relish — "and, oh, some more khir, Rani Saheba, it's so very grand" — etc., etc.

The Elder Raja Sahib has his long hookah and offers it even to Europeans when they come on a visit — he does not mind their smoking with his own pipe. Strange the way men are made. I suppose they are made that way. They talk of other women before you as if you were but just the mother of the heir, or a goddess for worship. They'll buy you pearl necklaces. The trouble however starts when the child does not come. For every chit and slave a child is born, as if it grew on the backyard banana plant, but for Rani Rasomani (brought up with such care in Darbhanga — her father was the younger Raja there) this lack of child within the year was sin. Yes, it was sin. And she consulted astrologers, and they gave her talismans. This too brought no result. She started visiting sadhus and they gave her sanctified rice and asked her to fast every Monday and go to Mathura, Prayag, Benares. But before the young couple could start on pilgrimage he died. He fell from a horse visiting a ricefield and died in Bankipur. In those days it took a night for a telegram to come. It took ten hours for the train. The brahmins 'rought his ashes, and she went with these to Benares, and she never returned.

The peculiarity of the situation however was just this.

In Benares she discovered she was going to have the baby. A posthumous child is no child some said: it had not known the touch of its father. But the father-in-law was a Brahmo, and all that. He behaved like what the Europeans did. He gave her an estate, a mansion in Benares —

> Hé, make way ye strangers,
> The yoke is meant for the bull,
> The womb is meant for the baby,
> The string is meant for the lute,
> And the string is meant for the lute —

The palanquin bearers now rest the palanquin on its supports, fan themselves with their turbans and shout: Hé Shambho!

> The string is meant for the lute
> And man is meant for worship,
> Hé Shambho Shankara.

and the crowd joins with the palanquin bearers and cries out,

> Hé Shambho.

Yes, a daughter was born. "O you high-chatterer," shouts one of the palanquin bearers, as he sees a huge monkey on a roof wanting to find the precise moment to jump down and steal the bananas and coconuts, on the silver, ritual tray before the Rani Sahiba, and the monkey grins.

The daughter was called Himavathi[2] Devi because she was born in cold January. The astrologers of course declared her to be endowed with the eight riches of earth and heaven and she would marry a great man who would go overseas. Now that meant something. When you go

---

2. Himavathi means daughter of the snows.

overseas, for Rani Rasomani, you learn to drink and you are received by Edward VII. That this jolly emperor of India was dead long ago never occurred to her. To her nothing changed. Edward VII still ruled India. "How are things at home?" she would ask and the courtiers who came from Calcutta, knowing her said: "The elder Raja by the grace of the great gods is in good health and the younger ones are enjoying life's multiple riches and have many children." This ended all enquiry.

Make way make way ye strangers
Rani Rasomani is coming.

The truth is she'd forgotten even that she was called Rani Rasomani. When she heard her name it was as if she always knew it but did not know where properly to hang it. She had no teeth and her eyes were whitey dim. Yet her limbs were so firm she could almost leap out of the palanquin and step on the carpet laid for her before the temple. "The Rani Sahiba is come, the Rani Sahiba," the doordrummers would shout, and in a minute Pandit Shivanth would be at the temple steps with kumkum, flowers and camphor. She would rush up, would the old, old lady, to have a darshan of the Lord silently and people would even there, where Shiva was so gloriously present, never deceiving in life or in death, they too, the worshippers, make way for her — the Rani looked so lost and so imperious — the worship would be quickly over. Her brahmin servant Shanker Deo would then lay her carpet behind the temple yard, and you should see how she sits in meditation. She sits as if the thought was but one, and one only — a thought is a thought, so there is no thought. When she thought of Lord Shiva he was present to her, with the serpent garland, the tiger skin, the Ganges crown, his third eye filled with compassion. For her Shiva was real. More real she would say than this hand, and she will beat her exquisite hands against the marble of the temple floor to prove Shiva was Shiva.

Her Bengali was not very superior — she had never gone to school. She could read letters, and sometimes when the Pandit was not there, she read some Purana or the other, in translation. She was not wise or kind or foolish or ignorant: She was she. And even that she did not always understand. Her palanquin bearers she knew, and sometimes she remembered her daughter. Well, well, her daughter was no great problem for Rani Rasomani. Hima just did not exist. When letters came, for Hima and her husband were in England now. Bijoy had some job in the embassy there — he was a close relation of Lord Sinha's, and he had been in the army first, and now in the diplomatic service. Though he was not a bad boy his wife seemed to have taken to her father's ways: they say she drinks and she smokes. Now this does not matter you know: that's the way with posthumous children. They take after their unknown fathers. And the grandchildren are worse. They speak no Bengali. And when you do not speak Bengali you are about as civilised as a Paksar monkey. The English language is all right when you've to read newspapers or to say yes and no to Edward VII, but this invasion of an untouchable tongue everywhere was desecration. You don't say your beads in English, do you? Or can you say your mantra in that guttural, awkward tongue?

> Hé, hé, make way make way
> There's no road like the Benares road,
> No virtue like truth,
> There's no wonder that's not Shiva's gift,
> No beauty but chastity.
> Hé, hé, here comes Rani Rasomani
> Make way, make way, passerby.

The road back to your district is always easier, it would seem as if the gods had given wings to the palanquin bearers — they run, and do not care, and when beggars rush to the palanquin or an ekka swishes past you, there's always the running whisk-bearer, he shouts like Bhima, and his voice could be heard till the city clock-tower. Even cars go slowly past the palanquin as if a queen were passing by, and laughing, the shopkeepers decided and said: "That's the Rani of Kashi." And when Rasomani heard it — she was pleased. She was born in Benares or was she not? — did she not marry in Benares, say? and she will have her body burnt there too in good sandalwood — and as for the rest, the monies were already allotted to holy charities. Of course Hima has a rich husband, but one does not bring a pot of water to the flowing river, does one? The fact is for Rani Rasomani there was nothing real. All was Benares. And the only living being she recognised was Ma Ananda Mayee[3]. When Ma came to Benares, Rasomani Rani would go palanquin and whisk-bearers, to the ashram of the saint, and she would sit and sing kirtans. The Ma always blessed her the same way — gave her flower and fruit and spoke to her in clear Bengali. Ma had even given her a mantra, and had touched her beads.

Rani Rasomani was eighty-five years old, people said, hundred, said others, yet actually the astrologer would easily have told you she was only seventy-six. But she was so alone with herself, eating little (except some fresh fruit and this not too often) and saying her beads, having her bath, and going to the temple, and returning to her palace for the Mahabharata readings which had been read backwards and forwards within these last fifty years by the brahmins, while she dozes off in her chair, the peacocks keening on the lawns. The sacred-reading room lies just to the left of the veranda, so that she could stretch on her long rattan arm-chair by the entrance and hear the great ancient texts. Nobody comes to see her. Nobody does she go and see. The charities are looked after by the accountant Manna Lal. Life is simple. Even the drummers at the

---

3. The deeply revered contemporary woman saint.

gates have been sent away since the Congress Raj. This was done by Manna Lal one day, and the Rani Sahiba did not even notice it. ("Now," says Manna Lal, "you've to pay heavy income tax. The heaviest in the world, that's what newspapers say.") What?

So parrots live now in the drum-chambers, above the gate. What is Rani Rasomani then? Just somebody that was and is what was and so will be what is. One complicates existence with playing cards at Government House or being lost without the Edward VII cuff links (these the Rani Sahiba still remembers). She has now developed a passion for sandalwood. Huge sandalwood logs are bought — and they cost their weight in pure gold — so that when she will be burnt Benares will all smell holy. She felt no evil against anyone. She felt no love either. She waited for death as a baby-bird awaits its mother's beak, a gnat or caterpillar for food.

In Benares they say: Oh, she will live a hundred years. And I tell you she will. Just see her and you will know. To live a hundred years you must be a widow, wear white, visit Shiva's temple, and know of neither war nor of government.

IX

"Shambho Shankara," cried Shivlal as he woke on his thin, bankrupt bed. Bed was hardly the name one could give to his wattlemat, his much-holed mattress of sorts, and his tattered blankets three in all. The fact about the blankets, however, was just this — they were not all torn at the same place, thus you could move about in comfort almost anywhere on the bed without the Ganga ghat chill eat into your capillary system — for the Benares chill is like a carpenter's winch, it spins on itself, and pierces straight to the white of bone. There is nothing you can do about it, but just pray that warmth somehow come up the legs, and warmth does come up: "Shambho Shankara." And you seek out your beads; and with the flower-covered Shiva's head framed in your eyes, you start taking the great god's name. "Hé Shambho." And soon it will be time for you to go to your shouting Sadhu.

It's just the time the whole of Benares is waking up, for example that Shankar Shastri whose window you can see from your bed. He is always reading — for he sits at the window, and he has electric lights. You hear his door creak, and by now the light has disappeared — so it's going soon to be morning. The creaking of Shankar Shastri's door is dawn for Shivlal. It has a peculiar sandy self-confident crunch — as it if were a wall-lizard prognosticating, or, a forest mahua tree rubbing against an acacia, with the low morning breezes. For Shivlal came from the forests, and to him the forest was always home. Shivlal in fact knew little of man — that is of city man.

He came, did Shivlal, from Madhya Pradesh, somewhere near Chanda, and there you knew more about leopards, tigers and hyenas than you knew of city people. The only city man Shivlal had ever seen as a boy (and that was some fifteen or more years ago and, when they still had that big Eight-pillared House and the cattle in the yard, and the women at the querns — and this was long before the case had gone even to the district court, leave alone the sessions court) — yes, the only city man Shivlal had ever seen was a peddler selling golden bangles, safety pins, kumkum, turmeric powder, saintly literature, astrological almanacs, photographs of King George V and Queen Mary and of the Maharaja of Gwalior, with his full tiara and durbar regalia, and finally photographs of the Singer Sewing Machine — "And this, brother," he would say as if whirling the handle of the machine, with one hand, and pressing the cloth with the other, and making the cluck-cluck noise of the needle with his tongue, "and this brother can stitch your shirt in an hour, a bodice in half an hour, and a child's night-wear, and in any colour you like, before you've winked your eyes once, twice and thrice." The gentleman on the photograph, Mr. Singer, would agree, as though nodding his high, lean mechanical head but fifty five round rupees is for the majestic Grandfather, with his grave metallic voice, almost a month's tax payment to the treasury, and there are always the festivals, and the sending of choli-piece to the daughters, the bringing back in of the pregnant girls, not to speak of the ways of adoring and adorning the son-in-law, so that when you begin to think of it all, a joint-family household is more expensive than a single one, so said Father, even if you were rich and round in the first case, and poor and in your bed, by the Ganga, shivering as in the second. And then there is your uncle — but this came later. The city-man had, alas, to be sent away — his mouth cluck-clucking was such amusement for the children, yet if the Eight-pillared House people did not buy your machine, tell me, who else in this miserable village would?

Oh, yes, the village had a grand name: Vallabhpur it was called, and everybody knew there was a great Kakotia king called Vallabh, so Grandfather said, shaking the silver bangle on his arm, yes, Vallabh, the king — the same who built Saraswathi dam across the Narbada, and large canals and many temples (you can see these in ruins everywhere) and he built them when he had defeated the Muslims at some far off and forgotten battle. He also gave lands to brahmins in commemoration of his victory (victory cometh where brahmin feedeth, so the saying goes among kings), thus the Eight-pillared House came into existence, while another king conquered some other foe, and since Mangal Bahadur was a brave soldier, though a brahmin, and had killed a hundred foes with one scimitar, he was given this village in perpetuity ("till the moon stood high in the sky and the sun rose red and big every auspicious morn," read the stone inscriptions that still stood beside the courtyard well). Life you know is very simple. You kill one hundred people in battle, and you're given a village in perpetuity. That the village is tiger-haunted, a den of the hyena, the porcupine, and the teaser leopard, makes no difference whatsoever. When you say you have slain an hundred enemy-men you can kill a tiger or two as well. Sometimes the tiger cubs would go puling like puppies on the main street during moonlit nights — and you could see these through the barred windows — and I tell you they terrified you less than a visiting policeman. The visiting policeman needed a nice meal, an inner courtyard bed to sleep in (unless there was a willing woman somewhere down the village) and at least a piece of silver. But the tiger, he came — or she came as she went, and sometimes growled when she smelt a cow or a horse in the backyard. No tiger ever touched a man in Vallabhpur in all its history — unless you talked of that mad tiger of Bahadurabad or the old cronie of the Pusli hills — they of course took away babies or old women in the fields. Yet that is another matter. Tigers are good, you know, that is if you are good. And how many Gond[1] boys did not ride a tiger and he does nothing to them. For example there was Kishmish Singh, the Gond, who looked after the cattle in the Eight-pillared House. He, one day, sang a tiger to the water tank and made it go to the Shiva temple (he had such magic in his voice) and did not the tiger wave its tail and give a roar on looking at the god? The truth is: the tiger perhaps knows his Shiva better than you know yours, so said Grandfather, in explanation. The world is becoming so evil, he said again and again — in future all that will remain of Vallabhpur will be a few old men tottering in their forest coughs, a few aged widows, and the tigers of the forest coming to offer puja to Vallabheshwara, our temple god. Man is evil, today he loves his copper so much. He would rather his daughter married a tiger or your son a hyena than a proper human being, as long as tiger or hyena brought forth money, so to say.

Shivlal lying on his Ganga ghat bed had rehearsed again and again the events. First Grandfather's sudden death — he looked so like a tiger himself, but in death he looked a saint when they went to touch his feet, before they took his body away. Then the father's death — he died a few years later, returning after watching the workmen on his fields, he had dysentery and the rain had come, and you can't wait for the sprouts to rise — and no sooner the father was carried away and cremated by the river (amidst those tall flowing acacia trees), the uncle being the younger and having seen more of the city than any one had (and now he was, as it were, the master of the Household) — he put his nephews and niece, three boys and a girl, all on the streets. "There's much water in the river," he said to the weeping widow,"and much tamarind

---

1. A tribal people of central India.

on the tree, and the good God has given all the world for a home." Now, what had a poor woman done? Nothing except she be the elder brother's wife, and she ran the household. If she did it, not tell me, who else should? And the younger sister-in-law, of course, came from a house with a horse and carriage and many lamps on the veranda, and one cannot trust her, could you, like one does everybody? Besides they also said, she and her family were great worshippers of talismans and dark-mantras and marsh-creatures and the nail-driving-in-the-courtyard stuff. You had just to see how this Rudrabai pared her nails and put them away under your ears with many a secret saying, thus showing she was not to be trusted with your baby. And she painted strange unguents behind the lobes of her ears and on her pretty, pretty toes. Life is that way. And three days before *he* died, had she not, that youngsome witch, not gone on that dark night somewhere, and there were all those whisperings, soft steps, silences, and goings on. Yes, it was not dysentery — it was *they* that did it, the spirits. He had been frightened several times on the road coming from Sunderpur fair — and he was no coward. He saw shapes, faces, he said. He got fever again and again. And then the dysentery, and now the death. Who did it — *she*.

You see the uncle had a licence and a gun. He had been to the city and had learnt shooting. And since there were so many tigers hearabouts, and he had probably bribed Abdul Khan, the Sub-inspector of Police (and maybe they even went to the prostitute together), so came the gun. Now the important thing about a gun is just this: you've only to polish it every morning (with that evil smelling oil) on the veranda, and the whole village respects you. Not only the village but even the elder brother. Of course you stand up when your elder brother comes in, but at the root of your heart (and especially in the heart of that scorpion called Rukmini) you want the Eight-pillared House all to yourself. Already the Government Revenue Inspector, the Police Sub-inspector (a new one this time), the Cotton Merchant's agent Shiva Sunder Das, they all came, came to see him, and some even came in taxi-cars. One day they'd all come and be the guests of Maganlal, the uncle. Why should not one be rich, I ask of you? Why, there are so many rich people in Bombay. You could have a car, and have a driver to drive your car, and take your wife on a drive like the rich do on Malabar Hill, Bombay. Why should not civilization come to Vallabhpur. The first thing is to sport a western jacket, and buy your wife Bata slippers. With jacket and Bata slippers you can drink the best air God ever offered on earth.

Shivlal's father was too simple. He wanted to be (like his own father), a just and a true landowner. His younger brother, however, now dreamt of a cotton-ginning mill. *Koo kooo koooo,* the whistle would go and the machine would chug, and bullock carts waited at your door to get paid. The world is no more made for the plough and pounding pestle. Get up brother, and come to the city. A mill in town is the city in your pocket. And money would flow into the safes. Big people will come to visit you. And your daughter, now four years old, would one day go to the Hunter College, Nagpur (C.P.).

It's not so easy to buy a ginning mill equipment. You have to sell the land, and buy this tremble mumble machine. If your elders protest what do you do? You go on dreaming and scheming with your friends, in town. Friends indeed whom you meet at the drink shop or at Shanta Bai, the dancing girl. And big schemes were made. (The licence came, and the gun played its part.) There was not a man, fifty miles around, who could twirl a moustache, a gun between his legs. Everybody is not lucky. But does the gun always bring luck? What if it brought murder. Also when you have a gun you are with the British. When you are with the British alone can you win. Wars come and you go up. The picture of Gandhi on your wall is a disgrace for so important a landowning family. There was that big story of a murder in Bilaspur. A young widow was found murdered — she was found with a muslim lover. Communal riots were feared. You could patrol the streets now gun in hand (the Government allowed you to) and the whole district fell into your palm. Everybody feared you, feared anybody who'd a gun. From then on to the sale of the land (the brother gave in, he was so silent and good) and within a few months city cars came to stand at your door. Money came from everywhere. Who would not trust you now that you'd so many rich at your door. Meanwhile the rusty old brother died. So much less sneeze and cough in the world. An old fogey who lived as if the train had not been invented by man, or the aeroplane. The wife's makings must certainly have worked, too.

Maganlal (the uncle) occupied the whole house, and there was not a soul in the entire district who would save a widow and her four children from despoliation. After this the story is simple. The widow threw herself into the temple tank, thus she could haunt that sister-in-law (with Bata slippers and all, like a cinema star) forever. Ramlal, the elder of the boys, got engaged as a cook by the Dholpur Stationmaster and looked after the family, from afar, as well as he could.

One day (after long years of honourable service) Ramlal took the train (when his master was away visiting his family) — Ramlal, so one heard, became a cook on Malabar Hill, Bombay. (So much had Malabar Hill become a part of the Vallabhpur imaginationings.) Sankerlal the second son grew wise, and used to be a bicycle shop assistant, then married his boss's niece (the boss had no children of his own) and now dreamt of revenge, and motor cars. He is the only one who will not leave the district. Either that Gunman (that's what he called his uncle) is dead and cremated, or I. The father's death will be avenged. Now and again when the gay aunt comes to town, he stands at his shop door and shouts: "Hé prostitute, with which officer are you sleeping today?" For such things do happen, you know, and now that the mill is prosperous and the Gunman is all powerful, who can know where the money came from? But our Sankerlal too had made some money (in war-time the bicycle-taxi is good trade, you know, and the poor Gandhi-men need bicycles for the wide propagation of the Gandhi faith). And now the case will soon go up before Sessions Court. The lawyer Jagath Ram is hopeful. The British would anyway go soon. And under the Gandhi Government there will be no place for a wicked creature like the Gunman. The British will go, and we will have a just and non-violent raj.

The British have now gone, and it's so long ago. The Gunman became in the course of a single, single moon, a Gandhiman, and is now president of the Chanda District Congress Committee. His mills run better than ever — in fact he has three of them now. His wife wears high heeled slippers, and even speaks titter-mitter English, so they say. Their children go to convent schools, of course.

Shivlal, the last boy, was interested neither in the English language nor in the ginning mills. While living with his brother — the same who was a cook to the Dholpur Stationmaster — a Sadhu came in unobserved and sat on the railway station bench. "Fetch me some water, I'm thirsty," he said. The boy ran to the stationmaster's quarters (a squat house under the neem tree, there) and brought the Sadhu a glass of water. Meanwhile the stationmaster had warned the Sadhu: "Please leave the premises of the station, you hear. You cannot take the train. But if you do — I'll have you arrested." The Sadhu laughed: "Oho," he said, "try, and we'll see." The stationmaster meant what he said. Those were Government-rules, and the trains belong to the Government. But there was no policeman in eight miles circle. Anyway there was no need for a policeman either. The Sadhu just disappeared. The train came, stopped, emptied somewhat, and filled in with a few new passengers, and whistled — it was the Itarsi Express — but there was no Sadhu. At the time the train was just getting into motion, suddenly from the other side of the track, the Sadhu jumped on the running footboard. The guard showed the red flag. The train stopped and the Sadhu ran Kamandala and top-knot, across the fields, before they could find him. Shivlal was in tears. He loved the Sadhu. He loved the Sadhu's matted hair, and the marvels he told of his travels. Shivlal had even fed the Sadhu, at home, when the stationmaster was on duty and tied up at the station. The stationmaster was a young widower. His wife had just died. He had not married again.

The next morning something extraordinary was seen at Dholpur railway station. And people there remember it to our own day. When the Nagpur Express dragged in, one saw a Sadhu stretched on the farther track, with nails struck through his two feet and left hand, dead-down to the earth. Laughing, he was caressing his long beard, with the other hand. There was such a commotion, passengers rushed down, and some even fell at the Sadhu's feet, women fainted. But he was laughing away at the crowd, at the train, and at young Shivlal who was in tears. "And now," said the Sadhu, "make your train move. That wretched thing is nailed to this station as I'm nailed to this earth. Isn't that so, child?" he asked, looking at Shivlal. Shivlal would say nothing. He was sobbing. The passengers prayed: "Let me pay you the fare, Swamiji." "O come with me Swamiji, and be my guest?" "O Swamiji bless me, I'm an unhappy man. I have lost all my family in the recent Mahanadi floods." The Sadhu heard no one. The guard blew the whistle. The crowd ran to the train. The train whistled, and despite the Sadhu it started to move. The Sadhu swore. "You bitch," he shouted, "You move. I ask you: stop!" And Shivlal will still tell you at Dholpur station, the train stopped just after a few puffs like a kicked-in-the-shins cur. The driver, an Anglo-Indian, furnished and refurnished the engine with coal, pulled this plug and that: Chuk, chuk, chuk, it would puff, but it would not budge. And the whole valley could hear the Sadhu's laughter. Even more people jumped out of the train, and fell at his feet, "O great man may you bless us!" "O great man let me have a child." "O great man," said Ramlal, the stationmaster's cook running from the stationmaster's quarters, "May my brother win the high court case against that wretch, my uncle." This was before Ramlal had left for Bombay. The stationmaster himself came down with the guard. The guard said: "Sadhuji you could go to the end of the world as far as the Western Railways are concerned. But please allow us to go." The Sadhu laughing pulled off his nails as you would the firewood from the burning oven. The driver now whistled. And the Sadhu, his clothes, his trident, and his kamandala, slowly went as if in a saunter, towards the train. Many doors opened. Shivlal followed him. "Jump in, child," said the Sadhu. Shivlal jumped in, like his dog. And the Sadhu entered the compartment and all the passengers gave way and made a place for him, to sit. Some brought out a pillow, and others carpets, and a few lit incense sticks. Some offered him bananas. Shivlal was so proud. The Sadhu took the fruits and gave them to Shivlal.

"Where do you go, Sadhuji?"

"I go nowhere."

"But you must go somewhere?"

"All somewheres go to one where."

"But," said a clever passenger, "that somewhere must be some sanctuary, some spot, some riverside holy city."

"There's only one place such appointed — which is no, no place."

"Benares," said a pandit, his fingers trembling with old age.

"The city of Kala Bhairav is no place, for everything is destroyed there as it arises. So I go where there is instant destruction; therefore all is. Where Shivji danced on the crematorium is where the world is real. Time and space are burnt to ashes. To live, you must dance," said the Sadhu and gyrated in the corridor of the wagon and in such a manner that the passengers (and Shivlal too) thought he would just jump out, and fly away.

"Shiv," he said, "fill me now, my hookah." And Shivlal put the tobacco and pushed it deep in, and when the train stopped, some passengers brought coal embers from the railway engine, and laid them on the tobacco.

"Ah," said he to Shiv, "you're a worthy devotee to a Sadhu." And Shiv loved the Sadhu so much, especially the smell of the hookah.

The story is long. But the end is simple. Shiv and the Sadhu after many wanderings came to Benares. Shiv soon discovered that the Sadhu was no easy person to serve. "Oh, fill the hookah, get me a soda water bottle. Hé, go and find me three ripe mangoes, and then get me some milk. You say it's for Sadhu Satyadevji. Who does not know Sadhu Satyadevji?" Shiv discovered the Sadhu lost his temper easily, and when he did, he almost grew red-hot like an iron blowpipe fallen into the kitchen fire. The Sadhu also did not mind pilfering here and there, and if found out, he used such foul language: "Son of a prostitute, I'll sleep with your mother." And he'd threaten people with all and evil things. One day in Benares (after they had been some fifteen days on the Ganga ghats) Shiv was wandering aimless through the streets. He was in tears. The Sadhu had howled at him (the Sadhu had had no bhang for three days — nobody had brought it to him).

True Shiv was negligent in performing his daily, dedicated duties. But he was a landowner's son. And at the thought of Vallabhpur and the tiger cubs running through the moonlit streets, he bursts into sobs. A woman bejewelled, with much pan-red on her lips, and with temple offerings in her hands, and a gay gait, befriended him. "Son, why do you weep?"

"I'm an orphan," answered Shiv, "and I am homeless."

"Come and I'll feed you. And you can stay with me,"

said she. And she took him to a grand three-storied house and onto the second floor; when the woman came in Shiv saw there were lots of men in the apartment, musical instruments lying carelessly about the place. They all smiled and bowed to her, and some started tuning the instruments to play their music. There was also an old woman, tired, and with a husky voice. "Mother, I've found this orphan. I liked his face. We'll keep him."

"Well, you've had enough boys here. They never brought you anything, but misery. And why do you want one more hooker."

"Mother, I liked this boy. I think he'll bring in luck."

From that day onwards Shivlal stayed in that house and started on his new job. When foppish men come to the door downstairs, he must lead them in. Then disappear. And in a few days Shivlal could go anywhere in Benares, and when he found the proper men — he knew them almost by a second instinct — he would say: "Maharaj, I know just the place for you." "O, go away you heady bloke." "No Maharaj," he would insist, "it's not far from here. And she is so ripe. And full. And the music so good." The more the man threatened the more he wanted to go *there* — this Shivlal, by now, knew. So Shiv would some times play pranks with the future customer and say: "O you are searching for the Rukmini Temple or you want to buy a maina and the cage," and the man would smile back and say, "I'll skin you, do you hear. Go away." But whether you want neither, a caged maina nor the Rukmini Temple, you still come to Gowalia Lane. The Benares concubines are famous through history. How come to Kashi Vishwanath and not taste of the honey of consecrated womanhood? "Lord, may she be handsome, and may she know love-making of such a wise, the earth knows no greater truth. Lord, the woman is the most beautiful thing you have created. The breasts and the waist, and the music that rises, curls, and falls, — and her dance is the dance that the Lord Shiva himself initiated mankind into. Takkadhim Takkkakakaka dhim, ta dhim — and she dances. Look."

> Takkatakka takka
> My love is like a twisting creeper and there she goes twisting her waist, and showing her ripe breasts
> My love is cool like honey
> My love takes me where no light goeth (But to where all love is — and here she gives a long wink)
> My love is tender as betel
> My love stays where I move,
> And moves when I stay.

Shiv learnt some of these songs too. And he became such a raresome success, that other women said: "Shiv, if you came to me, you could have ten per cent of it." Others came — but one fat Punjabi bitch said: "You stay here and take all the money. You are the lord, and I the slave." And Shiv somehow fell to the fat bitch. He brought her men, and juicy big men, too, and she enjoyed them, and they enjoyed her, and money just flowed into the house, as never it had. Shiv forgot his tiger and the cubs. He was better off now than in Vallabhpur. That wretched uncle might have mills and cars, but here Shiv is no poor hanger-on. Policemen visit him (to have access to pleasure or money) and sometimes even politicians. There was one big politician, who in his hurry, forgot his Gandhi-cap in the house. Shiv now put this headgear on and he looked ever more respectable. The Gandhi-cap gives you such respect that you could go anywhere, and nobody will say one harsh word to you. It also made contact easier. A Gandhi-cap trusts another Gandhi-cap. And when two Gandhi-caps meet there's much greater fun. Life is not worth living now, I tell you, unless you speak the Mahatma's tongue. Of course the British have left, that was so long ago. They left, and we have swaraj. But this juice of woman, what could life be without it. Hé, what do you say to that, Shiv?

"A woman's juice," quoted Shiv, "is like a river that stavs."

"You're a wonderful man. Where do you come from?"
"From Bombay," lied Shiv. He hated to speak of Vallabhpur and the Eight-pillared House. "In Bombay I learnt all the tricks native and foreign. Yes," continued Shiv, "and the white woman has no juice. Did you know that?"

"How so, mosquito mite?"

"Why, how can there be juice where there's neither the smell of turmeric nor of the civet bone. The woman's treasure is in studied smells," he said and rolled his eyes in such mischief, the Gandhi-cap just followed him.

The fact however is: Shiv had never touched a woman. Evil though the Sadhu was he'd given Shiv a mantra. The repeating of it was simple. It gave him power over desire. He also sang hymns morning and evening — the Kalabhairava stotra, the Chandi stotra, etc., etc. It made every woman seem so like a mother, all women were creatures rising out of the lotus stalk, wearing garlands round their necks, crowned with celestial diadems, chanting sweet hymns. "A woman is beauty," he said. "A woman is creation. A woman is sister. A woman is mother. I worship all women." That's how Shiv felt. He made money, and much money. And this went on for many years. He kept it in a tight heavy trunk of steel he'd bought in the bazaar. And whenever he'd time he'd slip into the Annapurna temple, and sit in prayer. He prayed that he be kept pure. And he went far and deep into himself, but he knew not where. And coming back he'd bring a client for Nanna, for that was the fat Punjabi bitch's name. She was so good, she was always smiling, and so virtuous. She was kind to the poor, she was friendly to the rich. For her money was important. Yet so was the satisfaction she gave man. She wanted no false money. Every man she satisfied God would remember, and she would have that much credit in her next life.

Shiv respected her. After all she was born a concubine and she performed what she was born to: her dharma. An ass's son is an ass, a buffalo's son is a he-buffalo. What was wrong about it anyway. Take the name of Shiva or Rama and sing hymns. Truth is only in the holy name. That's the only truth which is truth.

One day Nanna said: I hear you muttering a mantra all the time, why don't you teach me one? "It's a Sadhu who gave it to me," explained Shiv, moved by the woman's big heart. Sincerity is not given to everyone, you know. And she insisted — and she persisted. "Oh, son, give me that mantra of yours? Please, please." So Shiv went back to the Ganga ghat, after these many years, and of course there he was our Sadhu, as full of fun, of bhang and abuse. "Nice son of a widow, to leave me in the wedge, you donkey's son," and he swished his trident towards Shiv. Shiv slipped and ran and laughed. And the Sadhu and Shiv pursued each other like boys, at the hoothoothu game. Hoothoothu, hoothhoothu, hut! But Shiv was so agile, though now a man, for the Sadhu to catch. Even the monkeys on the railings scratched their bellies, and seemed to enjoy this spectacle. When the Sadhu was out of breath, he said: "Stay." And Shivlal stayed. He made the hookah and filled it with chillum, the Sadhu had never had a better smoke. You could see from Shiv's fresh face that he had not forgotten his mantra. That works, you know.

The woman now came in search of Shiv. Whensoever anyone disappears in Benares you always find him or her with a Sadhu. And a good woman has quick intuition. Nanna found him with the Sadhu and said: "Little big brother, you've abandoned me." "No," said Shiv, "you wanted a mantra. I came in search of my Sadhu. He gave it to me. Take it from him." The Sadhu never said a word. He put his tongs in his burning fire, and looked at it several times, as if he were going to brand her. "A woman who sells her body," said the Sadhu, "is like the crow that lives on funerals. Both live on bodies. Woman do you see that pyre, there? That's the end to this pus and bone booby, a booby doll," he said, and showed his own healthy body. "Maharaj," she begged and fell at his feet, "give me a mantra."

"Come on the fourth day of ashad. Fast three days before that. Come without having spoken to anyone. Come and we'll see." And she was so grandly pleased she rushed to a sweetmeat shop, and bought back some pedas, and a few garlands from the flower sellers. The Sadhu tore the garland and threw the flowers into the river, giving away the pedas to the monkeys. He gave one piece of peda however to the woman, with a look of contempt and harshness, but she looked as if she'd been given royal gold. "Your trunk is where it is?" she said, did Nanna to Shiv. "No one will touch it. But since you've gone the business is slack." The Sadhu said to Shiv: "Go and help her." And Shiv wondered at this. Shiv still wonders.

He went every morning to the Sadhu and cleaned the ghats and cooked the meals, and after his own bath and meal he went off to Nanna for the afternoons. The Pakistani refugees too came to Benares, and for some reason they always seem rich. When they came it was fun, they were so jolly.

The money in the steel trunk must have been big, big. "What will you do with all that money?" Nanna asked Shiv once. Shiv laughed and said, "Oh, I'll go back and buy my Uncle's house, and his mills, and buy myself a wife." "Oh," says Nanna, "you will never leave your Nanna, as you'll never leave your Sadhu." But when one talks of money Shivlal seemed so self-absorbed, as if he were calculating. But one day he took the trunk to the Ganga ghat. He left it under the tree, by the Sadhu, and did not care. And on Divali night when the lights were all ablaze, and all Benares looked as if the city were seen in a dream, he opened up the trunk and started tearing the notes one by one carefully, piling pieces on a side, as if he were tearing splinters from a firewood. The Sadhu coming back from his intestinal duties saw this. He too joined this festival. He took every note and blew at it as if to purify it, and tore it all into more pieces than had done Shiv. The Sadhu now went down to have a bath in the Ganges, and still Shiv was doing the job. The Sadhu joined him again. By now people had gathered round them. Who can do anything in Benares that all do not want to see? If no one sees, the monkeys are there to see, always. The monkeys too got intrigued. This young man is playing some trick (for you may not have heard the Benares monkeys know as much as you do of the smell of money).

Deliberately and silently the Sadhu and Shiv had torn all the notes except a few hundred rupee ones. Some one fell upon them from the back and yet another, and another again. In the scuffle a young man was wounded, and many howled. And by the time the police had come the trunk had disappeared. But on that well-lit auspicious night Shiv and the Sadhu sat by Mother Ganga and threw each bit of paper one after the other, into her waters. And the papers hissed as they entered the water, thus did Shiv celebrate his Divali.

Few days later, Nanna came after her fasts. She was given the mantra. Shiv never goes to Gowalia Street anymore. But he's always so happy to see Nanna when she comes. Nanna is like a great big rock. Its beauty is that it is so firm. The more you look at it the more you wonder at God's patience in creation.

X

*R*anchoddoss Sunderdoss was a jeweller in Bombay. You can still see on Girgaum Road the yellow painted shop-sign, discoloured, hung high, the shafts and wheels of a dilapidated brougham lying all about under the young pipal tree in the front yard, and a little shrine, jut out of the garden walls, for the passers-by to worship at the idol of Panduranga Vithala that Rukmabai a devotee had seen arise before her just there, and in almost transparent marble, with flute, chest-jewel and white cow — and this must have occurred at least two or three hundred years ago. Even now on every fullmoon night women come to worship the deity, for it's he that gave a baby boy to Rukmabai, so legends say, to this simple woman who could not go to Pandharpur on pilgrimage (her husband was too unbelieving and pice-miserly to let her go) — thus the little children's clothes that hang all about the door — for God alone gives, who else would give, tell me? And many a lady in Bombay even now has a child only because of this Pandurang of the Girgaum Road.

Thus it was, the Sunderdoss family finally decided, and during the good Queen Victoria days, to build a small temple around the idol of Pandurang and organised regular kirtans in ashad — to be precise, on the rounded fullmoon day of the month, to commemorate the vision the Lord gave to Rukmabai, this humble devotee. On that day the Sunderdoss family, for generations, have worn heirloom gold (sometimes even new-fashion jewellery), that the god not forget the merchants that do "give and take" business behind his temple. And so good is our Pandurang, he never forgets his neighbourly worshippers, nor does he forget the owner of Krishnabai, the cow which is fed by the passerby with a handful of green grass and for an anna. Since the marble cow would not eat the grass, this cow will in the name of the Lord, and many an office-goer husband returning from his toils would beat his cheeks before the deity, and offer the cow her anna worth of graze. And at festival times of course, you had more worshippers, and the grasscutters had a gay time. They too prayed for a son, and some had more than a son given by Pandurang Vithala. Of what worth a woman's womb that does not bear a toddling heir? And some middle-class women in gratitude even bought two head-gears for the child, and hung one at the sanctuary, while the other was taken home for the coming baby. And every baby who wore this grew to be intelligent and wise, and often won the first prize at the Anglo-Marathi High School, off the Gowalia Tank. Sometimes, a kind father coming back from his office remembers his baby's first birthday would be the next Friday or Tuesday, and he just enters the Sunderdoss shop (under the new signboard, encrusted with silver and in Marathi, Gujarati and English characters, right over the door: Sunderdoss & Sons, High Class Jewellers. Shop Founded in 1799) to buy something for this coming celebration. And one of Sunderdoss' brothers, Bhagavandoss, the elder, Ramadoss the younger, or Ranchoddoss the in-between (all clad in muslin dhotis, their little caps still in velvet and filigree), would take you in, and seating you on the pillowed seats, show you every type of silver waistband — those with a serpent's hood, those with the lionman's head, or those with just in-turning screws. You could now buy the little silver tumblers or milk-feeders for the baby, also in silver, and in addition, a ruby nose-ring for your wife if you were so tempted. And around the first of the month the Sunderdosses took in one of their cousins, Madandoss, to help them — such the crowd.

Ranchoddoss was not really very different from any other member of the family. He was hard-working, devoutly honest (a lie on earth costs a kingdom in Vaikuntha — heaven, his mother used to say) and was a genteel husband. He had two elderly sons, one nineteen and the other fourteen, and a daughter called Sudha. The boys were good at school, and so was the girl, though she went to Saint Mary's Convent School, off Pedder Road. The bus took her to school and brought her safely back. Sudha was always the pet of Ramaben, her mother, and, "Sudha do this," and "Sudha do that" ran like a thread amidst the noises of the household, for all the brothers lived together, and their children as well, but Sudha was the most loved of all. She was also the youngest. They say on the day she was born suddenly a peacock, wings outstretched and keening, strutted past the courtyard (the mother had gone to Kathiawar, to her own mother, for the childbirth) and everybody said: "Well, this girl, she will bring in holy riches." However no gold-lotuses rose in the backyard fountain on Girgaum Road, but money came in more and more — the Maharaja of Bhavnagar sent his own Dewan for the nephew's marriage, and since the purchases went over a lakh of rupees (and those were the true old days when the rupee was still worth its weight in solid silver) and the honesty of Ranchoddoss impressed the Dewan so greatly, the Rajas of Gwalior and Indore came along, and even that American wife of the old Indore Maharaja. Sudha brought prosperity no doubt, but Sudha who was so full of song and fun, suddenly grew serious, as the women's things on her chest arose, and she would hide her face behind pillars, even when her uncles and cousins passed by, or on her bed lie covered up with a light white sheet, all day. She hated talk, and she began to go less and less to school — but who cares? — a girl is meant for marriage as a wheel is destined for the cart. You don't use a wheel for a ladder or for hanging your clothes on, do you? The wheel is meant for a chariot, a bullock cart, or even for a brougham, like those wheels rotting at the housedoor as there is no spring or axle to wheel the box. And all that European talk of women going to become politicians or professors is so much like making the river run backwards back. Of course you can make the river run backwards through canals, etc. But when the floods come, the dam and the sluices and the canals are washed away as so many cold weather leaves — so too the woman.

Yes, Sudha was very much a girl — a woman, in fact, for she was fourteen years of age, and she hated marriage. For her marriage (and all the girls at St. Mary's Convent School, only talked of boys and marriages) was something stupid, no, more than stupid — sinful. "Why touch a man?" was her problem. Men seemed to her (all except her father, her uncles, her brothers) either awkward or evil. One never understood from where she got this idea — some said later it's the way the Christian girls talked of boys, or it's after she started going to films, and it's the European films that did it. Sudha, however, sat for hours on end in the family sanctuary, repeating the Name of the Lord. "Rama, Sri Rama," she said and went on naming His Name a thousand times, and little by little three thousand times, a day. She even started on fasts and days of silence, and sometimes took a vow to name the Name-of-Rama a lakh of times in ten days. She grew pale but beautiful. The family did not worry — she was after all only fifteen.

But one night, however, a few years later she had a real vision. In three days, it revealed, a sadhu would come to initiate her, and she would then become a true devotee of the Lord. Indeed, as foretold (and she had told no member of her family of this vision, except it be to her father, whom she revered), a handsome looking sadhu, hardly thirty five years of age, came into the house. He was a man from the South, and was, so he explained, on his way to Badrinath and Kedarnath in the Himalayas, and then finally he would come down and go, he would, to the holy city of Benares. "Passing by this street, Mother," he said to Ramaben, "I could *see* some sincere soul was living here. Is there anyone living in this house who's deeply devoted to the Lord?" Sudha, who was inside, knew this was the saint whose arrival she was anticipating, and throwing away her bedsheet, and coming out, fell prostrate at his sacred feet. "Too long have I waited for you," said the Sadhu. "Where have you been?" — "You, Lord, know more than I do," she whispered back in reply. The Mother could not understand. But Sudha suddenly remembered, so she explained later, all of her past life. A large house, somewhere in Kathiawar, or was it elsewhere? They spoke a strange tongue. She was forty or fortyfive years of age, and had raised four or five children. And they were gay and prosperous, horses in the stables and elephants in the yard — some men went to the wars, others played cards or roamed with women, but her husband suddenly died and she then knew she loved him more than she did God Himself. Her husband was, though a prince and real Rajput, the worshipper of a great Guru. For every sneeze and scratch he would run to the ashram of his Guru, which was on the marble cliffs of our beautiful Narbada. She did not care for God. But once her husband had departed, her one thought was he, and her union with him. How noble it was in the old virtuous days: you could be burnt with your spouse, your Lord. It's a pity the British came and stopped it all. She went back to the same ashram on the Narbada. But the Guru had, by now, given up his body. His disciple who had succeeded him gave her a secret mantra. She repeated the mantra again and again, and vowed she would find God now that she had no husband. She died however without seeing God and not even having an intimation of His Holy Presence. She died beautifully though (she could now see her own funeral procession) — people throwing flowers on her bright, elderly, saintly figure.

And she was then born to Ranchoddoss, and when the time came, the past life returned too, if not tell me why this hatred of marriage? Her Lord of one life was the Lord of all lives. And there he was. He knew. She "saw". And he stayed on in the house, and in a way the whole house became a roundabout for him — the elders said even the business was suffering because of this Sadhu. After three months, on an auspicious day Sadhu Sunderanandaji (for that was his name) initiated her with the full consent of Ranchoddoss and Ramaben, to sannyas. She put on the white sari, and a few days later with her sadhu, she departed for the Himalayas. Her family did not weep — they were too grave to weep (except the mother, who said, "Lucky I am to have borne you, my daughter, but Lord give me peace of mind. I cannot live one day without my daughter"). However the household moved on as before except that Ranchoddoss began to look more and more like his daughter, talk like his daughter, and he also began to fast and festivate for this and that. The business nevertheless prospered. His two sons Govinddoss and Vithaldoss were honest, devout and money-minded. Now and again when the business was not too bright, he would open to Vishnu Purana or the Bhagavatham, and read chapter after chapter of one of these sacred texts.

One day it would be about the Krishna and the gopis, from the Bagavatham, or of the Goddess Laxmi, rising out of the milky ocean, on a stalk of blue lotus, and this from the Vishnu Purana. But the story he loved most of all was of that king, who having lost interest in his splendorous world, suddenly comes upon a deer with its young in the forest, and he brought the little one home, petted her and fed her, but when he died he was, of course born a deer, for remember, you are reborn as your last thought be. And again, as a deer he was so wise and sparse of need, for he well remembered his past life, as king, but was born again as a man, and a brahmin this time, a brahmin fat and big, uncouth and repulsive, saliva dripping down his cheeks, and destiny made him, though a brahmin by birth, a palanquin bearer of King Suvera. But so indifferent was he to everything, and bore the palanquin so unequally paced the other palanquin bearers shouted at him again and again, when finally the king himself jumps out of his palanquin, and asks in royal ire, "Who are you? And why do you do this to me?" To which the palanquin-bearer brahmin replied: 'Look, Sire, I am fat and strong, uncouth, saliva running down my face. Look, look at me, but tell me, King, am I my face, my limbs, my nose that dips this snot, am I, I? Tell me truly, who am I?" Then he told the king of his past lives, which he remembered so well, and of the king who loved the little deer so, and of the deer he was born as, and again of the brahmin he is now. "Who indeed am I?" And boldly asked of King Suvera: "And how shall I denominate you, Sire? Are you your body? Who are you, king? And, what, pray is a king? Tell me, please, what is an object? Is this a palanquin? Of what wood however is it made? Do you know its name, and whence it came, and where sawed out, fixed, and made into a palanquin?" And the brahmin finally said, "just as the universally distributed air, going through the holes of a flute, makes for the variegated melodies, with sariga, sariga notes and all that, yet all this is but one piece of bamboo. There is no I, there is no you." And so saying, he suddenly saw within himself then and there as if jumping out of his person, — thus, he was forever freed from birth and rebirth. And so too did the king. Ranchoddoss told this story again and again to himself. He related this story to his wife Ramaben. "The truth is just that, Rama." But she could find no satisfaction in such legendary talks. After all she was a mother. And how can a man, any man, understand that?

Some years went this way. However, Ramaben could never console herself for the loss of Sudha. When sorrow grows it can grow big as a fruit in the belly, and even pushes out thorns as a cactus does. She suffered as no one had seen people suffer. The doctors gave her radium treatment, but she died one morning, however, very peacefully. She would at least have a better life next time, decided Ranchoddoss, wiping his tears when he came back, with his brothers and sons, from the cremation grounds. One has only to get there, where there is neither birth nor evil death. Is that not so, Sudha?

And now that the two boys — Govinddoss and Vithaldoss — were married, and the elder brother and younger, Bhagavandoss and Ramadoss were both alive and prosperous, Ranchoddoss left home to seek his daughter. And he found her without difficulty in Benares. You can ask any brahmin in Benares, where anyone else is, and somehow they will tell you, or take you to another who will tell you, all you want to know, where your daughter is, or your uncle. And he will even tell you, not only of all your ancestors, father, grandfather, and greatgrandfather, their names all written down in their family documents, but also of your jewellery shop on Girgaum road, and of Panduranga Vithala, who appeared to Rukmabai, because she could not go to Pandharpur, in addition to the flute, white cow and peacock crown. All, all we know. Such indeed the brahmins of Benares. For, remember, what you find not bad and good in Benares, you know you will see no such truths any elsewhere on earth. Here, in this most sacred city, I can tell you, whoever wants to hear that in final wisdom, there is neither virtue nor vice, for both burn like those pyres on the ghats, equally — to ash. Don't you understand this? Even the curs here know it.

So, led by his Gujarati brahmin guide, Ranchoddoss found Sudha in a little brick and mortar hall off Hanuman Ghat, where she read the Vasista Ramayana to widows and ascetics and to a few retired judges and ex-Congress ministers, and in fact to anyone who wanted to hear this great advaitic text. And as it should happen, Sudha, on that afternoon when Ranchoddoss beheld his daughter, — she was reading the story of Utpala the King. She just smiled, lifting her head, when she saw him entering the hall, right at the door, yet went on steadily reading the text. You remember the story, don't you, of how Utpala was a great King, a good and moral king, following all the eight rules of reigning a kingdom, that is — to be generous to brahmins, to be just, be wholly devoted to his subjects, slept little, kept all the castes under the holy laws, strict with women, kindly to children, and a great worshipper of the sages. And once when he was asleep, in his Hall of Slumber, he had this strange, strange dream. He had gone off on a hunt and had wandered far, leaving all his retinue behind, and how it happened, he could not remember, but that he was lost in the depths of a forest. He came across a hut where an untouchable was curing the carcass of a bull, outside in the courtyard. When surprised to see himself there, he was on the edge of asking the untouchable, in which province or hamlet he found himself now, when he espied a maiden fair. On course he immediately fell in love with her, and married her, and in good time she bore him a son. The years passed, years on years passed, and one day, the Prime Minister appeared, and asking said: Your Highness, we have searched for you all these times. We have searched this whole vast forest. But grace be to Shiva, we have at last discovered you, and when he was, the king was, returning back to his kingdom, he woke up and found himself on his bed in the palace. It was a dream after all. But it was deeply real. He was fully awake in his dream, just as he now was. Who was he, the king in the dream? And the untouchable and the beautiful wife and the son? Who is to decide, which is real, asked Sudha lifting up her head, smiling: who indeed? The story implies only this: Those years after all were but a few hours of one night. Life is just that. Behind both is the absolute reality, Brahman. It takes but the time a thorn takes to pierce through a lotus leaf to know the truth, — so Vasista, the guru, declares it to Sri Rama, understand! It is beyond Kala, time, and Desa, space. That Reality, Sri Rama, is you, is I, said Vasistha, the great sage. And of course Sri Rama understood and immediately too for he was, Sri Rama was, is the Ultimate Reality itself. The waking state and the dream state are both states equally wakeful. What is beyond that, continued Sudha, is no state: It is the I, the I, she repeated. Ranchoddoss thinking of the king and the deer, and the brahmin and the king again, yes, that is it, she is right, he said to himself. Sudha seemed indeed to Ranchoddoss, learned and very, very wise.

And as they walked through the busy lanes of Benares, finding a room for her father, she told her own story. Her Sadhu had passed away a few weeks earlier, she almost whispered with swelling tears in her eyes, and he had been asked by his own Guru in Badrinath, that she, Sudha, should carry on the reading of Vasista Ramayana. She was happy, she said, of her early morning baths at the Ganga, and her visit to the Shiva temple, off Harischandra Ghat, where she sat, under the ancient pipal tree behind the shrine, first saying her beads and then in meditation for four hours in rapt solitude. And then she went home to the Dashashwamedh Ghat, where in a three storied house by the river, she had a large room. At her door, she explained, her followers always left vegetables, rice and firewood. She would cook her food, eat and come after a brief siesta, to the hall of the holy-readings. An oleograph picture of Shiva as Pashupathi, hung on the wall, in the middle (as Ranchoddoss had just seen) with the sacred-seat, garlands and oil-lamps and all. Under the picture of Shiva, she would spread out her volume of Yoga Vasista, and after a brief bhajan, she would begin her readings, fixed for the day, adding her own humble commentaries on the text. She was no scholar, she explained, but she understood, because of the Grace of her Guru, the nature of what people say is the most difficult of all things in philosophy — Shankara's theory of Mayavada. "Father," she said, looking at the flowing Ganga before her, "Father, I think I have just a chink to the door of Knowledge — to Jnan." And then she went up to her room, laid her book and beads on the sacred table, before her Guru's picture, and offering her deep salutations to him, came down, and gently said; "Father I have not heard of the news from home. Is everybody well? I forget all about them here. But what is there to remember, anyway, and what to forget?" She looked at her father, and on the falling evening, she saw a tear on her father's face. A street lamp revealed it. And she understood.

Her father took a room next to hers, it was at Vishal Nivas, on the sacred Ganga of course, and by the Dashashwamedh Ghat, and he too began his meditations. She gave him just a few hints, because she was no Guru, and then one day a few months later, he and the daughter went up to Badrinath, to see her Guru (that is Sadhu Sunderanandji's Sat-Guru) and the Guru after many words of praise for the daughter, gave initiation to Ranchoddoss. He asked Sudha's father to read Sri Sankara's *Upadesha Sahasnyam*,[2] and come back to him again, and in a year. Life flows as you see, like the Ganga herself, simple and abundant, carrying princes and dancing girls, fishes and carcasses, the pyres burning on her side, reminding you that the Truth is but one indivisible flow. What is dream and which reality, then?

So that Ranchoddoss now lives in Benares, and I assure you, you cannot miss him: always as neatly dressed as in his shop, with his muslin shirt, and his dhoti falling in precise folds, sandal paste on his brow, courteous to passers-by (and Benares is not known for courtesy, as any grandmother will tell you, especially by the ghat sides). And each dawn he will wake, and saying his beads he will go down the ghat to the River. There, like Sudha, he bathes

---

2. A thousand instructions.

and sits on the steps for meditation, and returns to his room to cook. Once in a while the postman will have thrown in a letter from his family, or some Maharaja he'd known in Bombay will seek him out, asking him silly questions of philosophy. What does Ranchoddoss know? He knows nothing. Only Sudha knows. But Sudha will not help a Maharaja become more virile (she knows of no such miraculous mantras or trichurations) nor will she bless them that they get back their kingdom — they made such an ugly performance of it all when they had their ancient thrones, some indeed which had come down from the time of Sri Rama. Once in a while a Bombay professor or Kathiawari aristocrat will come and ask Sudha real and earnest questions. She will answer them all, even about the serpent and the rope, or the dream and waking states. And some even in that obscure nature of the deep sleep state. Sudha is happy. Ranchoddoss as you see is proud, and happy.

You can still see him sit on the bank of the Ganges, as the evening begins to fall, and, as the temple lamps begin to leap from tower after tower, and the gongs begin to extone, clapping his hands gently, he will sing Shankara's,

mano nivrittih paramopa shantihi
sa tirtha varya manikarnika cha
jnana pravaha vimaladi ganga
sa kashikaham nijabodharupaha.

The cessation of all mental activities is the supreme peace — that is the holiest of all holy places of pilgrimage, the Manikarnika (in me); the ever-flowing stream of knowledge is the pure primeval Ganges (in me); (thus) I am the Kashika, of the form of pure Consciousness of Self.

XI

The power of man is to sow, the berth of woman to reap. The bullocks may plough the field, the birds go plucking bugs and berries through trees, the shout of man come through all of space as if in a known straightline — the elephant will browse by the railway platform, the camels carry tight perched burdens on their humps, but the river's flow is like a name — it shines through its own insistence. Boats ply as in a silent dream, as though time and movement were one, but space the meaning of sight, and all of human geste but a play on oneself. Man is not a beast of burden but a song to sing, and the earth a temple-garden where we sow what we pray. For prayer is life, and life breath and substance, that men wean not away from truth. So that every word is a sacred name and every name a true sound. Let us hear the *anahata*, the heart-sound, that we know ourselves, and that the river flow.

What if the river should stop, Lord? (Like once she did, you remember, when you held her thunderous flow in your topknot, the moon smiling above her) What might the Vedas do then, and the fishes and the seeds and the sounds and the elephants? O, let water flow, Lord, that the earth turn not away from its fulcrum, whirl, earth, that the Ganga flow, round and around on herself, from earth to sky and from the heavens back to the Himalaya. The circle is the end of all beginnings as the Ganga is of water.

For, where the flowing ends — *ap*, the is-isness of water begins. So, now Ganga, flow.

Death has no meaning. Man's approbation is for the true. Sit with me and let us listen. The river has depth, and, see, the birds have flight. The boat has eyes, and the bridge its leap. Yet must man wallow with the donkey or the child play with flies. In the gullies of Benares the smells are exuberant, the ladies' shy — shyness curves their saris to bent innocuity, but man's passion is in the starved shine of his eyes. The gutters go their way making time, carrying little broken claypots (that milk and tea and curd have used for man's satiations, and that ritual purity has destined for their formal destruction) — the gutters have broken baskets, little threaded sweetmeat trays, an ant-eaten umbilical cord, torn sackcloth on which bees sit for a better taste of funeral honey. The gutters leap through the side streets, open up by corners, and gay they go half-full with dark moving fluids to any Ganga Ghat, and leap down under pipal trees. For all of here must be holy, and even the sewage has to rush in cascades, and be hallowed by the pipal's knotted roots.

Man's illumination, however, is of the mind, yet he shapes his utensils for proof of his material disposition. I am a pilgrim, so I have a pot. One pot. Big pot. Small pot. Brass pots with tusk-beaks or silver ones with swan-heads, pots with cow-mouths or pots with just arches carrying handles, pots are pots and the Ganges has no choice. You dip and you bring it to your pilgrim room and wax-covered, you take it back home to Maharashtra, Bhuvaneshwar or Rameshwaram, and place it securely in your sanctuary, by the flower-covered gods. Ultimately, when the time comes, you ask your son, uncle or grandfather for the Ganga-*jal* as you begin to heave a heavy breath and you sputter yourself in, and now move into immortality. But the problem is, how immortal can you be? For that matter the dog that floats down the Ganga is even more immortal. Its mortal body is all afloat on the Ganges. And that of drowned pigs as well. You, dark and bloated pig, you know you too are immortal. Life is a grave game, oh, ye brahmins. You talk so much of immortality. It is all a contribution to your purse. The mantra is money. The temple bell is for begging. The puppy's yell is for the mother. Mother never gives birth to a child for all end at the Ganga Ghat.

The puppy sits on that ash and dungheap and cries. Its one eye is sore. Flies do not leave him in peace. So, he cries for his mother. The donkey, above him, finding no cucumber scrap to chew shakes its head to wave off its flies, and tries to suck the puppy's ears. But the donkey's flies prefer the larger ear. And somewhere there a child's undershirt lies in flowery rags. Whose child might it have been? How tenderly its mother must have pressed him to her rounded breasts. The rag is a sign that in life's finality nothing matters. The fact that you live at all is the miracle.

For, in Benares the living are the miracle. They can walk on their bamboo legs, their lathis and their turbans proving their strength — in Benares men even talk. Whence did they get their strength? For their silent moving mass is like those toppled palaces, their own platform self-sustaining above Ganga's rubble — a tree shoots from that ruin to prove life's insistence, but by the next flood the platform will also fall to the depths from which no one will ever retrieve its stones. The maharajas have all gone, anyway, you must remember. Empires have fallen thus. Indeed all of structures' destiny is decay and disappearance. The fact of existence is just this — action and reaction. Action and reaction again. Why should one be born? Why should one sorrow? The turrets and carvings of Benares architecture seem to name life as real, yet only death appears to shine here as true meaning.

Son, has death meaning? No, death is an empty event. It's like the yawl of a crow, the son of a barren woman. Can life die, that is the question? The Ganga answers: Man, you think you die. Burn yourself on my banks and know that what flows cannot but unflow. Death is a superstition, like the flies that sit on the baby's rags, and find nothing there. Is the donkey's bray a song? How can you, who have a name, die? If the Ganga cannot grow dry one will never know death. Hence is she, the Mother of compassion.

Man is mortal is the grandest fib man ever invented. Foolish is man in trying to believe in such a lie. When knowledge, as Ganga, as jnana-ganga, flows, death is dissolved into truth. She is, as Sri Shankara said: She is nija bodha rupa, she, the form of Consciousness pure.

I do not know why I came here. Raja is a name given to the nameless, as wave is for water, as sound a name given to volute silence. Why then should I be here? How could I be here? Where is the here, where I am? A point is no space. Nor do a series of points make space, as a series of perceptions make not an object. The object is not in seeing but in perceivingness. There is no here, Lord, there is no space, no movement, therefore I am the Ganga that flowing flows not. For where ends the flow? Nowhere. Where there is no end there is no beginning. Anything that is non-existent at the beginning and also at the end, does not exist in the middle either, says the Great Gaudapada Acharya. He was, as you know, the Guru of the Guru of Sri Shankara himself. Thus, you fool, realise; the Ganga never flows.

How simple is the truth if only we listen to ourselves. But we prefer to listen to the crows on the Ganga Ghat, to the chatter of brahmins at the funerals (and in our temples) and to the ekka drivers (who frighten you with talks of death and taxation) and to those dead to death, the sadhus. The fact of the fact is simple. One cannot go to the Ganges. One cannot go to the "I". For if you dare have a deep look on the Ganges evenings, and see the Ganga unflowing, then you know there is no Ganga. Water is just water. So, O, Mother Ganga, please be gracious, and, — flow.

Notes and Glossary

ashad: Hindu month (June-July).

bairagis: Extreme ascetics, often known to torture their bodies, to show how indifferent they are to the flesh.

bhang: An intoxicant.

bhayya: Villager.

brahmachari: Celibate.

Brahmo. Also *Brahmo Samaj:* The great Hindu reform movement which started early in the nineteenth century, and fought against idol worship. Keshub was one of its well-known leaders.

charpai: Cot.

Dashashwamedha Ghat: Where traditionally ten horse-sacrifices were performed by Brahma according to tradition, when Brahma himself beheld the Shiva Linga for the first time. It is one of the most popular ghats of Benares.

dewan: The Prime Minister of any princely state.

dharmasala: A resthouse for pilgrims, where usually one can stay for three days without paying any rent, and one is even sometimes supplied with food from the temple or the charities during that stay there. A very ancient custom available in most parts of India even today, especially at sanctuaries.

Divali Festival: A festival which takes place in the October-November, no moon day of Kartika and is in celebration of the Lakshmi, goddess of wealth.

ekka: Horse cab on two wheels, which reminds one of the ancient chariots.

Ganga: The Indian name for the River Ganges. Traditionally a celestial river comes down to earth in compassion for human suffering. Her descent on earth was to be so powerful that Shiva had to hold her in his topknot, lest she destroyed the world. She is also the daughter of the Himalayas. A bath in her is supposed not only to wash away our karma—the accretions of all our past lives—but also free us from rebirth forever.

ghat: Steps of stone leading to a sacred river, stream or lake.

gujarati: Of Gujarat, one of the classical provinces of traditional India.

halva: An Indian sweet dish.

hookah, hooka: Hubble-bubble.

jellebies: An Indian sweet.

Kalabhairav: The dark hued Kalabhairava, an aspect of Shiva who has the dog as his vehicle.

kamandala: The bowl of the Sadhu, often shaped like a human skull or may be a real skull of man.

Kanhia: Familiar name for Sri Krishna. Yasodha was his mother.

Kathiawar: A part of Gujarat state.

khir: An Indian sweet dish, prepared from milk and rice.

kirtans: Hymns singing groups.

lakh: One hundred thousand.

lakhpati: Someone who owns hundreds of thousands of rupees.

lathi: A long wooden pole used often by peasants as a walking stick, and for defence against wild animals and robbers.

maina: A pet singing bird akin to a lark.

Manikarnika Ghat: The last of the five famous ghats of Benares. This is where everything—that is creation—began and this is where also, it ends—thus the well of Vishnu, the creator, and again the most celebrated cremation ground, where everything ends, for each one of us, the circle ends—as whatever begins must also have an end. Hence the sanctity of Manikarnika Ghat, where having dipped into Mother Ganga, you now go to the Lord of Benares, Lord of Kashi, the great Vishwanath, the Supreme Being, of the Universe that is He, the Pure Being, and so the "I". The "I"—aham, in Sanskrit, means the indestructible *(na hanyate iti aham)*. Thus the indestrcutible "I" of Shivoham, Shivoham—I am Shiva.

mantra: Magical vocables—like the sacred OM—which, formulated by the great sages, have immense spiritual power for inner growth. It is akin to an incantation, but has to be given by the Guru, in ritual initiation for effectiveness.

mayavada: The philosophy that the world is not real or unreal but a delusion. Like saying: the son of a barren women or horns on the head of a hare.

Pandavas: The five brothers, according to the great epic, the *Mahabharata*. The *Mahabharata* is not only the longest epic in the world, but is also the most popular not only in India but in all southeast Asia. It is about a war between two cousins, the Kauravas, the usurpers, and the rightful heirs to the empire, the Pandavas. These were five brothers: Dharmaraja, Bhima, Arjuna, Nakula and Sahadeva. The two last were supposed to be twins.

Parvathi: The wife of Shiva. She is the daughter of the Himalayas, who being in love with the ascetic Shiva had to do a long penance to win him as her Lord. She is the compassionate aspect of Shiva, the Truth.

pativrata: In the Indian tradition, a chaste and devoted wife is believed to have almost divine power.

peda: An Indian sweet.

pheni: An Indian sweet.

pice: The lowest denominator in erstwhile Indian coinage—made of copper.

Prasad: Offerings to the gods, shown to them and returned by the priests at the temples.

rajputs: The heroic fighters, because of whom one part of north India is even today called Rajasthan. It might be said, a Rajput is a hero or nobleman. He belongs to the kingly caste, that of the kshatriyas.

Ram Lila: The festival of Rama, when the whole of *Ramayana* is enacted, with new players, every year.

sadhus: The ordinary peripatetic mendicant friars. There is officially almost one sadhu for every hundred Indians.

sannyas: Ascetism.

sannyasi: A wandering monk.

Shiv-Shivah: Meaning both Shiva and his spouse, Parvathi.

Shiva: One among the Trinity of Indian Gods, Brahma, the Creator, Vishnu, the Preserver, and Shiva, the Destroyer, who prepares the way for Creation. He is perhaps with Sri Krishna, the most celebrated of the divinities of India. Sri Shankara's famous Hymn on Nirvana, ends by saying the "I" which is attributeless, and so unborn and deathless—this "I" is Shiva Himself: Shivoham. Shivoham. Benares is the city of Shiva.

siddha: Highly evolved ascetics who are supposed to live in the mid-heavens.

Sri Shankara: The most revered sage of modern India. I say modern for contemporary India has been mainly shaped by him. He was the most celebrated philosopher-sage after the Buddha. He wrote most of his texts as commentaries on the Vedas and the Upanishads. He re-established the basic non-duality in the Indian tradition. The date of Sri Shankara's birth and passing away is still an unsettled matter among scholars. Historically he was supposed to have been born towards the end of the seventh and passed away towards the beginning of the eighth century A.D.

swayamvara ceremony: Choosing of a bridegroom in princely families, when in an assembly of neighbouring princes, the princess puts a garland on to the one whom she chooses. Bhoja Rao and Vikramaditya are famous ancient kings of the Indian tradition.

Tulsi Das (1532-1623): The famous poet of north India, who wrote (like Dante) in the vernacular. His most loved book, *Ramacharita Manasa* (The Most Holy Lake of the Mind—the Story of Sri Rama) is more read and heard than any other book in the whole of the Gangetic plain. He lived in Benares, and finished his great poem there. Mahatma Gandhi used to read it, during his later years. In some ways it is, after the *Bhagavad Gita*, the Song Celestial of India.

Vishwamitra: One of the most important sages of the Indian tradition. He is always there to help something to happen: to create or solve a crisis.

Yama: God of death.

zamindar: A traditional landholder, often owning land given by the rulers because of some distinguished military or civil service to the Government.